Peter Minto

STAY LUCKY

TRAPPED BY AN OFFER HE CAN'T REFUSE – AND A GIRL HE CAN'T RESIST

Peter Minto

STAY LUCKY

Trapped by an offer he can't refuse - and a girl he can't resist

MEREO
Cirencester

Mereo Books

1A The Wool Market Dyer Street Cirencester Gloucestershire GL7 2PR
An imprint of Memoirs Publishing www.mereobooks.com

Stay Lucky: 978-1-86151-454-7

First published in Great Britain in 2015
by Mereo Books, an imprint of Memoirs Publishing

The address for Memoirs Publishing Group Limited can be found at
www.memoirspublishing.com

The Memoirs Publishing Group Ltd Reg. No. 7834348

The Memoirs Publishing Group supports both The Forest Stewardship Council® (FSC®) and
the PEFC® leading international forest-certification organisations. Our books carrying both the
FSC label and the PEFC® and are printed on FSC®-certified paper. FSC® is the only
forest-certification scheme supported by the leading environmental organisations including
Greenpeace. Our paper procurement policy can be found at
www.memoirspublishing.com/environment

Typeset in 12/18pt Bembo
by Wiltshire Associates Publisher Services Ltd. Printed and bound in Great Britain by
Printondemand-Worldwide, Peterborough PE2 6XD

To Christine (Kit)

CONTENTS

CHAPTER ONE

Saturdays were dead days. Experience had taught Steve Cromarty that nothing ever got started then, and too often there was time to reflect on the lack of success during the previous five days. But this Saturday was different. There were two messages waiting for him, and there shouldn't have been any. He'd only been in the flat four days and he certainly hadn't left a forwarding address when he'd made the move. As far as he was aware no one should have been able to contact him here, not even Jill. He'd spent the night at her place; a good night in many respects, although, considering she was a company secretary, he'd assumed there would be a bit more from a business angle, and that had been a distinct no-go.

It was just after 11 am when he returned to his flat. The letter from the bank lay face down on the mat just inside the door, its embossed logo seeming to mock his attempt at disappearance. Just for a moment as he turned it over he thought it must be for the previous tenant, but it was not.

He tore it open. There was no beating about the bush – no niceties, no 'Dear Steve' as they would once have addressed him, simply a curt 'Sir'. And then just the bare facts; he had three days to bring his account into credit.

He shrugged; disturbing though that was, he could live with it – he had in the past. But the second note was altogether different. It was inside his flat, pinned to the frame of the door into his living room where no innocent visitor could possibly have gone. Written with a ball-point pen on cheap lined paper, it said: 'Birmingham Trade Fair, tomorrow. Bertram Imports – JUST LISTEN. Could/should be of interest to you'. There was no signature.

It took only moments for Steve to check the doors and windows; there was no sign of an illegal entry. He pulled the note off, took it into the small, inadequately-furnished room and poured himself a small Bruichladdich. It was far too early, but he needed to consider the implications calmly, and the whisky would help. He'd taken the usual precautions to keep his whereabouts secret. Obviously the bank had found him, but so had someone else, someone who knew how to bypass the Royal Mail.

Of the two messages, the one from the bank was on the face of it the more threatening, but the pinned note gave him far greater concern. He checked again for possible signs of a break-in or any disturbance of the few possessions he had there; nothing. He then thought of his smooth bastard of an estate agent, but he grudgingly sympathised – these were tough times and he would have to pull in what cash he could when he could.

He threw back the rest of the whisky, but decided not to have a refill. Someone not only knew where he was now living but had access to the flat. They were also aware of his line of business and, it seemed, his urgent need of an earner. Why they should choose to give him a helping hand was beyond him, but he didn't see what he had to lose.

He decided to take the advice. After all, his business affairs depended to a large extent on following up rumours, suggestions and ill-advised confidences. Hanging around trade fairs, with or without legitimate invitations, had been part of his modus operandi for more years than he would admit to.

Another aspect of Steve's routine was his morning workout, and he saw no reason to allow one or two unbidden notes to change that. So for the next hour he put aside all other thoughts and proceeded to push himself through his own pain barriers.

It was half an hour past noon when he dragged himself out of the shower and towelled himself dry. He knew from long experience that the general fatigue in his muscles would take at least two hours before it would gradually recede. The question flitted through his mind, as it seemed to do increasingly often these days, as to why he still bothered to put himself through it. Twenty years ago it had been an essential part of his job, but that could have been a lifetime ago, or even someone else's lifetime ago. A wry smile creased his face.

He stood in front of the full length mirror. Forty-six years old, six foot two, thirteen stone and not even the hint of a paunch. He nodded approvingly; he was no Narcissus, but as he looked at his reflection he knew the answer to that question about why he continued to punish himself, and turned to retrieve his clothes. He could still score where women were concerned. Jill would vouch for that.

He just wished that his financial affairs were in as good a shape as his body. For far too long now he'd been fending off increasingly impatient bank managers who were showing the same lack of faith as his wife had in his ability to pull off the big one. She'd eventually gone her own way. He had probably been more relieved than she had, as the relationship had become an irksome charade. But bank managers – they were something altogether different. It was vital to have at least one sucker on your Christmas card list, as in his line of business, ready access to funds was essential.

That brought his mind back to the second note. He had good reason to follow it through and make the trade fair at Birmingham a priority.

★ ★ ★

The following Tuesday Steve was at the South Terminal of Heathrow airport. The Alitalia Flight 134 to Pisa had been boarding for fifteen minutes when he made his way up the steps and received the welcome smile and complimentary morning paper from the stewardess. He found his aisle seat and settled down, ostensibly to read the paper but in reality once again to run over in his mind the reason he was heading to Northern Italy.

The trade fair on the Sunday had been the usual mix of expenses jaunt and social drinking, with just sufficient in the way of business presentations to justify the event. Normally Steve would have done the full circle, as he knew the importance of keeping a good profile among as many groups as possible. But this time, because of the note, he had focused on one group only. For a while it had looked as though he was wasting his time, as nothing of importance was coming his way – until…

It was little more than a whisper, and to anyone else it would certainly have gone unnoticed. But to ears tuned to the right wavelength, it was a thundering great shout. And Steve Cromarty was on the right wavelength.

The word was that Italy was the place to be. "With Berlusconi in it's all systems go for risk takers, but with far less risk there than here," said the top man at Bertram Imports. Anything coming from a man with his credentials had to be taken notice of – big notice. Steve was not one to miss an opportunity by spending too much time considering the possibility of drawbacks; he was prepared to chance his arm, particularly now.

However, despite all his best efforts, there had been a galling two-day delay before he got fixed up with a flight, and even then it was only because the Alitalia desk girl was a friend of a blonde he knew in Daventry. However, looking on the positive side, he took this as further confirmation that Italy was the place where it could all happen. Or to be more precise, the city of Florence, which had been named by the whisperer. Steve had a gut feeling that this could be the big one he was looking for; the Big Screw – capital B, capital S – that he'd been so tantalisingly close to in the past but never quite collected on.

If he had seen the last passenger to board the plane and known that four days previously that same man had made a special trip from Florence to Birmingham to brief the chairman of Bertram Imports, he might not have felt so confident about the successful outcome of his trip. The man, tall, heavily-built and bearded, sat several rows behind Steve. Three hours later when they landed at Pisa's Galileo Galilei airport, he made sure that he was off the plane well before Steve. By the time Steve had yanked his case off the heavy, rubber-slatted carousel and made his way from the airport concourse along to the railway platform, there would have been no sign of him even if Steve had been looking.

The train for Florence was waiting, ready to depart, and almost as soon as Steve had got himself settled, it pulled out. He gazed out of the window at an untidy urban sprawl that could have been almost anywhere, were it not for the garish modern art graffiti which took up most of the end walls of the drab blocks of flats that bordered the tracks. There were political slogans linked into the designs but, as his knowledge of Italian was limited, he found himself struggling to make much sense of them. He was just about to give up on it when the large, heavily-bearded man who had been on Flight 134 lowered himself into the seat opposite.

"Just one more wonderful thing that the Italians have given the world," he said in Italian, addressing the remark to no one in particular. Then he turned to Steve and said in English, "It's not the usual postcard view of Pisa is it?" He had the slightest hint of an Irish accent.

"I've seen better," answered Steve, wondering how it was so obvious to the man that he was British. He continued to look out of the window. If there was one thing he hadn't come to Italy for, it was to talk to an unknown Irishman.

For most of the rest of the journey Steve felt the man's

eyes on him, although there was no further attempt at conversation until they were pulling into the outskirts of Florence. Then the man sat up straight and for the second time inclined his head across towards Steve.

"Are you from north or south of the border?" he asked quietly, but this time there was no attempt made to hide the accent.

"Does it matter that much here?"

"It might," was the answer. He leaned back, looked intently at Steve's face, and then slowly closed his eyes. "It just might," he repeated, his eyes still closed.

The train had slowed to near walking pace and as the Santa Maria Novella station sign came into view and Steve pushed himself up and started to gather his things, the Irishman spoke again.

"If you're interested and feel lucky, try the Irish pub one night, I might be there," he said. He opened his eyes for just a moment, then shut them tight again and snuggled himself further back and down into his seat and into his beard. Steve ignored him, hauled his gear off the train and made his way along the platform and out to the station entrance.

He had only a few minutes to wait before a taxi glided along to take him the short distance to his hotel. In that time he realised two things: first, he was overdressed in the heat and glare that was bouncing off the walls and roadways; second, just before he got into the taxi he saw the Irishman standing in the shaded station entrance. He couldn't see his eyes, but he would have put money on it that he was watching him.

CHAPTER TWO

The delay of two days in England, although a source of frustration, hadn't all been wasted time. It was many years since Steve had been in Florence, so he had taken the opportunity to gen up again on its basic layout and then, perhaps even more importantly, he'd found out where Bertram Imports and others of like ilk tended to gather and when. This last had been due to Lady Luck smiling on him in the form of a junior executive who had been more than willing to talk of his big dealings over a few friendly beers. So Steve had booked into the Hotel Roma, which was where the taxi now dropped him. First impressions of the place, which was reasonably expensive and reasonably central, were very favourable – it would certainly do him for starters.

He had not formulated any particular plans, but that didn't worry him. He was more than used to playing things as they came; reacting to changing situations and making quick decisions had never been a problem. After checking in he left his bags in the room - unpacking could come later - and made his way out into the square. Chance caused him to turn right, and within fifty yards, he found he was approaching the Irish Pub. It didn't look like the sort of place where big business might happen, but for the first night he reckoned that business could be put on hold. Sampling a bit of Irish-Italian entertainment would not be unwelcome. What was it the bearded man had said? "If you feel lucky." Well perhaps he should give luck the chance. It could be no worse than having to down three or four Guinness.

He side-stepped his way past a cluster of parked scooters and a large group of young black people who were thronging that corner of the square. Then he was past them and into a mixed crowd; mixed nationalities, mixed sexes, but all of them twenty to thirtyish, almost filling the area immediately outside the pub's frontage.

Even as he pushed his way through the narrow, green door with the harp motif etched into its half glass, Steve began to wonder why he had bothered. This was an 'in' pub with an 'in' crowd and anno domini was not on his side. But once inside he knew he was committed; the only people going out were well laden with at least one full glass in each hand, some even doing a well-practised balancing act with two in each hand, one above the other.

His doubts were immediately swept away when he reached the bar and caught the eye of a very attractive red-headed barmaid. He decided that he might as well order two pints of Murphys while he was there; drinking room inside was at a premium, so he'd have to take his drinks out, and he didn't fancy having to force his way in again. It also gave him the chance of some conversation with the barmaid while she pulled pints directly in front of him.

"Is it always this busy?" he asked, having to lean across the narrow bar counter to make himself heard above the general noise of people talking and laughing and the amplified sound of the Dubliners.

She glanced up at him, and he took in the grey-green eyes, the fine skin with beads of perspiration and the low-cut blouse moulded around firm breasts.

"I think so, but I'm only here on Tuesdays and Wednesdays." She smiled and looked straight into his eyes as she pushed the full glasses across to him.

"What do you do the rest of the time?" he asked, thinking he could do worse than have this colleen helping him to while away any spare time he might have here.

She flashed her smile again as she took his money.

"I have one or two friends," she answered. Not for one minute did Steve doubt that. "But in any case," she continued, "it's too busy for me to talk. The boss wouldn't like it."

"And is your boss here tonight?" he asked.

She nodded and directed her eyes past Steve. "Over in the corner. With the beard."

Steve turned and looked over the heads of the milling crowd and saw the man who'd spoken to him on the train. No wonder he'd recommended the place.

"Your change."

He turned back and her teasing smile seemed to hit him. Without doubt she was stunning. In fact she was the most beautiful female he'd run into in a long, long time.

"He's also my father," she added. Then she was away from him to serve at the other end of the bar, leaving him wondering if that was just a 'hold it there' ploy.

He picked up his two pints and glanced across to the corner again, but the bearded man had either gone or was hidden by the crowd.

By careful manoeuvring he managed to get himself and his drinks outside. The plastic seats spilling across the wide pavement were all occupied, but just beyond them he found a convenient low wall to sit on. It was a pleasant, warm evening; just the evening to sit and watch the world go by, if you were so inclined. The square was full of people, most of them tourists; some were sitting on the cut lawns ringing the fountain, others were strolling along the Via del Moro towards the river or heading for the Duomo down the Via de Trebbio. There was also the group of blacks he'd passed on his way to the pub. There were no women among them, and that and the fact that they were all wearing expensive suits made it look like the gathering place for a convention.

A deep, Irish accented voice startled him.

"Did you come here because you were interested, or because you felt lucky?"

Steve had been so absorbed in looking at the blacks that he hadn't been aware of the bearded man lowering himself down onto the wall beside him.

"I'm always lucky," he answered. "Don't you know that? I thought everybody did." He gave one of his well-practised 'trust me' smiles.

The bearded man nodded slowly, his face completely expressionless while his eyes stared into Steve's.

Yes, I had heard something on those lines about you," he said.

"Who from?"

"Let's say a mutual acquaintance." He pursed his lips before adding, "And I happen to know you need cash, a lot of it, and quickly."

"Now just hold it there boyo," said Steve, putting his drink down very deliberately. He reckoned his image could do without that sort of tarnish.

The bearded man placed his hand on Steve's left wrist and gripped it with surprising strength. He smiled, but the words he hissed out from between his teeth didn't quite match up with the smile.

"Don't give me any stupid shit talk," he said. "I'm not a patient man. I know more about you than your mother ever did, or your wife, or the blonde you've been screwing in Leicester for the last two weekends."

He released his grip.

Steve glanced quickly round but no one seemed to have taken the slightest bit of interest; this was Happy Time, Florence-Irish style, and the young folk around them were not going to waste any of it watching two forty-something guys holding hands and talking close. As far as the rest of the world was concerned, they were alone.

"Okay, so my bank account could do with an injection, but let's face it, whose couldn't these days?"

The bearded man simply nodded and remained silent, seemingly lost in thought or just enjoying the evening, as he gazed across the square towards the grey and white marbled façade of the Santa Maria Novella church.

Steve half turned to look across the square, aware that something had changed since he'd arrived only a few minutes earlier. Then he realised that the group of black people had gone, while slowly wandering across the area where they had been was a heavily-built, elderly man wearing a long, fawn overcoat and carrying a battered holdall. He watched the man make a slow, deliberate journey across to the corner of the arcaded Via della Scala, where he carefully settled himself on the stone flagstones under the first arch, stretched his legs straight out in front of himself, and pulled his holdall across his chest. He unzipped the bag, rummaged around inside and then pulled out a bottle. He cradled it gently in both hands before taking a long drink. Steve would have sworn that as he took the bottle away from his lips he looked across at them and gave an exaggerated nod.

The bearded man broke the silence between them. "A woman is going to come here, into this drinking area, in the next few minutes. She'll be coming from that direction." He inclined his head slightly towards the street leading past the church. "She'll have a large dog with her," he added, almost as an afterthought.

Steve glanced past him. Although there were several women walking in the right direction, none of them had so much as a Chihuahua in tow. The bearded man must have guessed Steve's unspoken query.

"Believe me, she's coming," he said.

Steve realised then that the tramp's nod hadn't been meant for him at all, but had been some sort of signal to the owner of the pub.

"So what do you want me to do, hump her or the dog?" he asked, trying to bring a touch of lightness into a situation that he felt was moving out of his control.

"You won't touch her for a start, at least if you're sensible."

"Okay, so it's the dog then."

"That's right, it's the dog. Once she's seated and got her drink I want you to call the dog across to you. It'll have a red collar and there'll be six numbers stamped into the leather. All you have to do is memorise the numbers, don't write them down, and then leave here straight away."

"And then what?" asked Steve.

"You'll meet me at ten and give me the numbers."

"Where, here?"

"No, that wouldn't be a good move. Annie'll tell you where. She's the barmaid who served you these." He nodded to the drinks.

"Your daughter, you mean?"

"She told you that, did she?" He gave a smile which this time seemed half genuine. "Don't believe everything she says."

"What's in this for me?" Steve asked as the bearded man started to lever himself up off the wall.

"Nothing or worse, if you balls it up," he answered. "Yeah, probably worse," he added as he straightened his back. Then, quickly bending down again so his face was level and close to Steve's, he added, "That was always how it was in the old days, remember? Get it right and we talk big – dollars not euros. Get it wrong and we won't be talking at all." He turned and, despite the crush of people, made his way rapidly back into the pub.

Steve stared after him, forcing himself to stay calm, although inside he was badly shaken. He took a quick drink of his beer, which was now warmer than he would have preferred it. How did the bearded man know of the old days? They'd said that was covered for ever. And there'd been more than a veiled threat in his final remark.

He turned towards the corner where the tramp had settled himself with his bottle and saw that the place was empty. For some inexplicable reason his concern increased, but there was no time for further conjecture as he now became conscious of a woman with a dog making her way into the outer sitting area. She moved towards a table almost beside him which somehow, despite the numbers of people, had miraculously become vacant. A blonde waitress immediately came across to take the woman's order, although everyone else had almost had to fight their way into the pub to be served. While the woman waited for her drink to arrive she glanced round at the rest of the customers, including Steve, but he had the distinct feeling that she was completely uninterested; her glance in his direction was through him rather than at him.

She was not a natural beauty, rather a fine example of what expensive clothes, hairdo, make-up and confidence can produce when they are working in harmony. Even at thirtyish this woman could turn heads. Normally Steve Cromarty's would have been one of those heads, but not on this occasion. His concern was the dog; a big, dark brown brute of a breed he didn't recognise but which had the typical mainland European sharp pointed ears. It was long haired, but as the woman slipped its lead he glimpsed a broad red collar. It too, after an initial shake of its massive head, looked around in a similar manner to the woman, as if it felt it was demeaning itself to be associated with such company.

Steve was not a born animal lover, but over the years he had trained himself to suppress any indication of fear that might encourage dogs to think he was a soft touch. He leaned forward, clicking his tongue and the fingers of his left hand at the same time. The woman either didn't hear him or, more likely, was ignoring him, but the dog was just about to lie down when curiosity got the better of it and it lumbered the few steps across to the wall where Steve was sitting. The woman was taking her drink from the waitress and, Steve noticed, making no attempt to pay – she was obviously more than well in with the management.

He ruffled the top of the dog's head, bent down and with his right hand reached for the collar. If it was tight this could be awkward, he thought, visualising himself being dragged around by a dog which was not best pleased to have a stranger's hand trapped next to its neck. His worry was unfounded; the collar was fairly loose and he was able to pull it round and feel where the stamped numbers were. With his left hand he parted the dog's hair to see them. They were perfectly clear: 74 71 82.

He read them twice and then, just as he was about to let go of the collar, he felt a small cylinder, no bigger than a cut-down pencil, on the inside of the collar immediately beneath the stamped numbers. In that millisecond of time, fifteen years of inaction dropped from him. Conscious thought didn't come into it; all that McKenna, Parkin and Macbride had drummed into him flooded back and took over. With one step he was over the wall and running for the nearest exit from the square, into the Via de Trebbio, with the two words 'distance' and 'protection' thundering in his brain. He skidded around the corner and slowed to a brisk walk, at the same time trying to bring his breathing under control.

Thirty yards down the street he became aware of someone swinging into step beside him. It was the man Steve had seen giving an apparent signal about the woman's arrival. He was still carrying his battered holdall against his chest.

As he turned to look at him more closely the man spoke. The voice, the eyes, were vaguely familiar, despite the ravages of the years. Steve was suddenly confronted with his past. It was Macbride himself.

"Nice to be back in business with you again, Steve," he said.

Before Steve had the chance to reply, the sound of a huge explosion ripped across the end of the street. It was followed by a moment's shocked silence. Then shouts of fear, panic and pain took over.

Macbride hardly reacted to the blast. "I think we should refresh our memories of one aspect of the line of business we're in, don't you?" he suggested calmly. Steve made no reply, but together they slowly and very deliberately retraced their steps. When they turned the corner the scene of devastation and carnage was far worse than Steve had expected.

"I wouldn't have thought it possible, it was so small," he said in a low voice.

"All due to the progress of science, Steve," answered Macbride. "Where would we be without it?" There was just the hint of a grim smile on his face.

They skirted the wrecked area. There were already some uniformed men on the scene trying to quieten the hysterical survivors before they could sort out where aid would be most useful. Even at a distance it was obvious that a score or more of the young drinkers were beyond help. Others were alive, but had had limbs blown off. Steve noticed that the wall where he had been sitting only minutes before was no longer there. Bits of plastic tables and chairs had been blown across the road and some had become lodged beneath a metal bus shelter. As they passed it on the way to the Via del Moro, Steve saw the torso of a long-haired brown dog, minus head and front legs, wedged under a twisted table top.

Police cars and ambulances with sirens wailing and blue lights flashing took over the scene as Macbride led Steve down the street, pushing against the general flow of people rushing to view someone else's hell. He took him through a door, number 11, between Liverano's menswear shop and Bacarelli Antichita. Inside was a shaded, grassed patio area and on the far side heavy, beautifully polished double doors gave access to an elegant, comfortable living room. Steve's case and flight bag were standing beside a massive, grey leather settee.

"Nothing against the Roma, but we thought you'd be safer here," explained Macbride. "Your bedroom's on the first floor."

"And where's yours?" asked Steve.

"On the street corner where you saw me. Not quite in the same league as this place, but it has its perks and they pay well."

"So what do I do now, kick my heels here?"

"Just enjoy yourself, Steve. Annie'll find you, but don't keep the man waiting."

Steve moved across the room to check whether his

luggage had been tampered with, and as he did so he heard the street door open and close; Macbride had gone, so there was no opportunity for further questions. He knew where he could find him if necessary.

He looked around the room he'd been given. An ornate bronze sculpture standing on a heavy sideboard at one end of the room caught his eye, presumably from the high-class antique shop next door. It was made up of four horses pulling a Roman-style chariot and the chariot wheel was a jewelled timepiece. It was showing eight thirty, and Steve was suddenly conscious of not having eaten since the in-flight lunch. Macbride had said Annie would find him, and he had an hour and a half before the appointment time; time to do some eating and some thinking.

CHAPTER THREE

Steve stood for a moment outside his new quarters, undecided as to which direction would be most likely to lead him to a reasonable eating place. However, as he glanced up the street towards the Roma hotel and the Santa Maria Novella square he could see that there was no choice; the decision had been made for him. The police had blocked off that end of the street with metal hurdles. In any case he reckoned he'd seen enough of the bomb scene.

He turned and walked the other way. The Via del Moro was one of those streets which exuded timelessness and refined style; it wore an air of age and affluence without any hint of ugly extravagance. For the most part it was large private houses interspersed with the occasional exclusive shop. The thought occurred to Steve that the owner of the Irish Pub, or whatever organisation he was working for, was obviously not short of funds if they could keep an apartment there all ready for eventualities such as this.

In a hundred yards he found himself at the walled bank of the river Arno. There were several couples ahead of him enjoying a *passegiata* in the evening sunshine, and he followed them when they turned left along the Lungarno Corsini. Two bridges upstream from there he could see the ancient Ponte Vecchio straddling the river with its clustered parapet of shops, and he began to get his bearings. This would do him fine, he thought. It would be expected of a business/tourist visitor. Unless or until the bearded man came up with a better alternative, that was what he was here for and he'd better play the part. However, deep inside he was beginning to accept the inevitable – he was being sucked back in, and this trip was not going to turn out as he'd hoped when he'd flown from the UK that morning.

Just before he reached the bridge he leaned on the broad stone wall bordering the pavement and spent a few minutes idly watching some scullers on the grey-green water skimming through the centre arch; not that his attention was fully on them but more on a jeweller's window which gave him a reflected view of the *fondamenta* he'd just walked down. He saw nothing to give him cause for concern.

He moved on. The crowd had thickened considerably here and no one appeared to be in any particular hurry. He took a dozen easy, slow steps onto the bridge itself, allowing himself to be taken along by the general flow.

Then he made a sudden turn and pushed his way back past some indignant foreign tourists. Ignoring their comments of disapproval, some of which he understood, he took a diagonal route to the street corner, where a huge blue banner was hanging the full length of a three-storey building, partly to hide some major renovation work and partly to advertise the building firm involved. 'You'll not be aware that we're there' it said in both Italian and English in bold yellow lettering. Couldn't be more appropriate, Steve thought, as he pushed his way behind it and then waited for anyone who might be trailing him to wander in after him. No one did.

The building was open, so he decided to use it. The whole of the ground floor had been gutted, and it was littered with the debris of demolition. Making his way round piles of stones and wooden beams, all numbered, he found a door on the far side, conveniently unlocked, which brought him into a narrow alley linking onto the mainstream route, Via Por. S. Maria. From there the crowd's flow swept him towards the Piazza Signoria, but just before he reached the square, along a narrow side street to the right, he spotted the sign for a *trattoria*. Closer inspection showed it to be sufficiently nondescript to meet his needs.

The entrance was simply a narrow doorway from which a spiral, iron-railed staircase led down into the single, long dining area. At the foot of the stairs Steve turned sharp right and pushed through a swing door into the cramped kitchen. Startled and indignant voices were raised, but before the chef and waiter between them had managed to explain his error to him he'd seen what he wanted – there was a fire exit door at the far end of the small range of ovens and hobs, and it had a staircase leading up to street level.

With the help of shrugs and hand gestures he gave his apologies and allowed himself to be returned to the eating area. He took a table convenient to the kitchen door and slightly in the crook of the stairs. The waiter, without any other customers who might need his attention, hovered as if expecting to have to deal with further eccentric behaviour from him. To calm his fears, and because time was pressing a little, Steve made a quick choice from the menu and gave him his order – a bottle of house red and *zuppa di verdure* to be followed by *agnello arrosto*. He poured himself a glass of the wine, thin but acceptable, and then began to try to make some sense of the situation he now found himself in.

Twelve years before, at the ripe old age of thirty-four, Steve had been a victim of cuts to Britain's anti-terrorism budget. In a world of changing power groups in Europe, Africa and the Middle East, a slimmed-down manning level had been proposed. As a result he was considered surplus to their requirements; 'of no further operational use' was the phrase they'd used. After eleven years of surviving in a world where only bastards survive – that had been McKenna's mantra preached into all of them, fresh-faced or hardened, at every retraining course – he was yesterday's man, past his sell-by.

"Who survives?" McKenna would bawl at them.

"Bastards!" was the chorused reply.

"What are we all?"

"Bastards!"

He could hear it ringing in his ears now and feel the adrenalin of self-preservation surging through his body as if it was yesterday, although he'd spent more than a decade trying to erase it from his system.

He'd been lucky; certainly luckier than most of the motley bunch he'd come into contact with during the early years. Most just weren't around any more – never would be. At least he was still in one piece and, although wild horses wouldn't drag a public acknowledgement from him, perhaps he had Macbride and company to thank for that.

Deliberately used as a stooge in the second of two abortive coups in Central Africa, to enable the British government of the time to wring its outraged hands and avoid embarrassing compromise, he hadn't exactly enjoyed the role of sacrificial lamb. Three years he'd been left languishing in various prison compounds in the area around Buta and then Yangambi before they'd had him shipped back home, ostensibly as a corpse – 'pneumonia' was written on the death certificate. Then another five years in various penal institutions as Steve Cromarty and his new civilian persona was set. On his release there was some money but living to make up for lost time, it hadn't lasted long. As far as his ex-employers were concerned it was a case of 'you're on your own mate' and 'nobody owes you a living, least of all us'. And for the last four years that was just what he'd done – this and that in the import-export line – until he'd ended up here, meeting up with his past in the shape of Macbride.

What use he could be to them now he couldn't imagine, but he knew that this wasn't coincidence at work; they didn't operate that way. He decided that he couldn't make any sense of it, at least until he had something more to go on, and that wouldn't be until after ten when he'd meet the bearded man again. In the meantime there was no point in taxing his brain cells; he might as well enjoy what he could of the evening.

At the end of the meal, which was adequate if not inspired, and the fact that it wasn't doing a great deal of trade seemed to bear out his view, he left and made his way into the square. On the far side the magnificent Palazzo Vecchio threw its imposing bulk across the scene, dwarfing the statues, even the fountain with the figure of Neptune rising from its centre. The whole area seemed to be awash with groups of tourists, mainly American and Japanese. The males were hardly able to walk straight, hampered as they were with their video cameras and all the attendant gear in various pouches strapped to their bodies. It seemed that for many of them the view of Florence would have to wait until they were back home running the video onto their TV screens. However, it did give Steve the opportunity to indulge in some enjoyable eye-catching with some of the women of the parties who were being left on the sidelines while their menfolk went in search of their unique, original, special view. It amused him particularly to hear one large-girthed American guy speaking over his non-camcorder shoulder, "Just wait till you see this back home honey. It's a knockout." Honey, who had obviously seen more than enough such knockouts and was looking bored rigid, had caught Steve's approving eye and was working her imagination over to see if there was any way she could find a spare half hour. She knew there wasn't, and Steve also knew there wasn't, so they had to make do with two sets of smiles and regretful, shrugged shoulders to indicate what might have been.

The time was now pushing on towards quarter to ten, and as Annie hadn't made contact yet he thought he should be making his way back to his rooms. He reckoned the Via dei Calzaiuoli, leading towards the cathedral and the baptistry would take him in the general direction of where he wanted to be, as long as he took a street off to the left

– he was one of those fortunate beings who had an inbuilt direction indicator which seemed to work in whichever city he found himself.

At five minutes to ten he was on the far side of the Santa Maria Novella square wandering slowly along in front of an hotel with a plaque informing the world that H W Longfellow had lived there for a while. But at that precise moment Steve's thoughts were not so much on the author of Hiawatha as when and how Annie would contact him.

He took the left-hand diagonal path cutting across the grassed area so that the several water jets of the fountain were between him and the Irish Pub which, although the bombed area had been reasonably cleared, still had a large number of uniformed police working there, together with several white-overalled forensics. Away to his right, in the corner of the first arch, he could just make out what looked like a pile of old blankets. He assumed it was Macbride, presumably huddled up with the inevitable bottle. Beginning to feel like old times, he thought.

He had just decided to return to his newly-allocated rooms, thinking Annie might have left a message for him there, when he saw her approaching. Her red hair looked even more colourful in the evening light and it picked out the red weave in the silk tartan shawl she draped across her shoulders. She was coming from the direction of Macbride's corner, but he couldn't say if there'd been any form of communication between them. She was carrying a small, white handbag. Half way across the square, she suddenly stopped, pulled out a packet of cigarettes, put one in her mouth, and then started to search in the bag, presumably for matches or a lighter. By then Steve was almost up to her and certainly close enough to see the pouting lips as they held the unlit cigarette. He gave an inward nod of appreciation. Her head was pointing down towards the open bag, but her eyes were looking at Steve and he saw now that the lashes were damp; she'd been crying.

If anyone had been watching her then her actions were exactly what one would have expected from someone seeking a light for a cigarette, but the words she blurted out to him bore no relation to her actions.

"You haven't much time," she said. "Mr O'Donnell wants to see you in room 114 in the Roma. But don't trust him."

Steve found a book of matches in his jacket pocket and struck a light for her before giving her the book.

"Why warn me, Annie?" he asked, as he cupped his hands round the flaming match.

"Maria, the other girl who was serving, she was my friend," she answered with a slight catch in her voice.

"Where can I…?"

A shake of her head stopped his question in mid-sentence. She passed the book of matches back to him, but before he returned it to his pocket he saw that she'd stuck onto it a small, yellow paper circle cut from a reminder jotter and there was a telephone number written on it.

"I think I might need you some time Annie," he said as they parted.

She nodded.

He continued on his way across the square, feeling pretty sure that the nod had meant more than just a legitimate end to their charade. He hoped so.

A police van slewed into the square and stopped alongside the bomb-blasted pavement area in front of the Irish Pub. The sight of it forced his thoughts from Annie to Macbride; a glance across to the corner arch showed that it was again trampless. For a moment he wondered where the man had gone, but then he forced himself to concentrate on the matter in hand – room 114 Hotel Roma and the meeting with O'Donnell, the man who was not to be trusted. Steve silently blessed Annie for her warning; O'Donnell was not going to have the monopoly as far as deviousness was concerned.

CHAPTER FOUR

Steve entered the lobby of the Roma for the second time that evening. The young man on the desk was not the one who had checked him in earlier.

"Room 114, sir." He had answered Steve's query almost before it had been uttered. "First floor, turn right from the elevator, or the top of the stairs if you prefer to walk up." It was said with what seemed to be a genuine smile – a hotel receptionist happy in his work.

From the reception desk the lift entrance was on the far side of a pink and white marbled column. The huge open lounge area was cool and opulent, with marble floor tiles and table tops. Several of the soft olive-green leather chairs and settees were occupied by well-dressed, affluent-looking guests. American speakers, they were loudly debating, of all things, the prospects of college teams in a round robin competition back home.

Before entering the lift Steve checked that the door,

and more importantly the illuminated floor indicator figure, couldn't be seen from the reception desk. The receptionist had looked just the sort of eager-to-help employee who would have tried to do something silly if he had seen Steve press for the second floor.

The lift was silent and quick. At the second floor Steve stepped out into the corridor and, finding that it was clear, he leaned back into the lift, stabbed the button for the first floor and then the door closure and left it to its own devices while he found the stairs and carefully made his way down.

'Needn't have bothered,' he thought to himself when it was evident that there was no welcoming party waiting for him at the lower level. Yet he knew that from now on he was back in that other world where you have to bother and be a bastard or you don't survive. There was no middle road, no choice, no options; it was permanent and he had to get himself back into the mode where it was automatic.

His knock on the door of room 114 was followed immediately by the sound of a clock inside the room beginning its ten o'clock chime. As the last chime faintly died away the door was opened by a young, slim Italian wearing an expensive, fashionable light cotton suit with shoulder pads in the jacket which seemed to reach halfway down his upper arms. He stood straight on to Steve, the expression on his face and his body language the epitome of arrogance.

"What do you want?" No sir here, nor a smile; pleasantries were obviously not his line of business.

Steve didn't have to answer, as the bearded man, O'Donnell, now appeared in the inner room.

"It's okay Lorenzo. This is Mr Cromarty, the man I've been waiting for."

Lorenzo seemed more than a touch put out that he had to move to one side to let him enter. Steve gave a flicker of a smile.

"Come in, come, in Steve," said O'Donnell in a voice which in other circumstances might have been considered friendly. He waved his arms expansively and led the way into the main room of what was really a luxury apartment which had French windows and a balcony looking out over the square.

"How does he fit into things here?" asked Steve, jerking his head back in the direction of Lorenzo, who was turning the lock in the door.

O'Donnell stopped and pursed his lips while he considered the question.

"You could say he acts as a sort of minder for me," he said.

"So I presume that's one of your jackets he's minding for you," quipped Steve.

O'Donnell, who had been making for the far side of the room, turned immediately and extremely quickly for a man of his bulk. Steve realised he was in a sandwich of his own making, with Lorenzo close behind and O'Donnell in front, all pretence at friendliness gone.

"Get rid of the jokes," said O'Donnell. This time the voice was more of a hiss, as it had been earlier that evening. "The Italians are not noted for their sense of humour, especially if it pricks their pride, and Lorenzo is no exception."

Steve was greatly tempted to make a remark about pricks he had known, but thought better of it. O'Donnell in any case was directing a stream of rapid Italian at Lorenzo, who answered in a high-pitched, disappointed tone, and then Steve heard the door being unlocked and Lorenzo left them.

"He might be very important to you some day, so it would be better not to ruffle his feathers," said O'Donnell, sitting down in an upright chair with his back to the window. He indicated for Steve to take the low easy chair which was alongside his. Steve chose to ignore it and instead leaned against the drinks cabinet. It was well stocked with Irish whiskies, suggesting that O'Donnell was a regular user of the apartment.

"Who might or might not be important to me hasn't been sorted out yet," Steve answered. It was an attempt to maintain a position, but already he knew it was simply a gesture of bravado; all the cards were in the hand of the man in front of him, and he reckoned they would be revealed in the next few minutes.

"Of course, Steve, the very reason you're here." He gave a huge, quick smile, but it had no effect on his eyes, which were hard and black and staring into Steve's. "Did you get the numbers I wanted?"

"Everything has a price," countered Steve, determined not to meekly submit.

"That's so true, so very true," said O'Donnell, in a tone of mocking sadness. "And the price could be a great deal more than you think." He tilted back in the chair, placed his hands behind his head, and stared up at the ceiling. "First," he continued, still staring upwards, "the numbers were 747182. Am I right?"

Steve could see where this was leading. He nodded very slowly. Annie's warning, 'He's not to be trusted', came back to him loud and clear.

"So you didn't bank on me playing it straight," he answered.

"Let's just say it was necessary." O'Donnell switched his gaze back to Steve, accompanied by the cold smile. Steve nodded again, his lips pulled into a tight line; he didn't much like the way this was heading. He moved across to the French windows, pushed the heavy, velvet curtain aside and looked out onto the narrow stone balcony and, beyond that, across the square. From here the front area of the Irish

Pub wasn't visible, but to the left of where he stood, and at a distance of no more than forty yards, he could see Macbride. He was having an apparently earnest conversation with a gaudily-dressed middle-aged woman. The sight of the woman reminded Steve of the question he had to put to this cold smiling, bearded, bull of a man, although there was no real need of a reminder; you don't forget things which have been burned on the memory. He allowed the curtain to fall back.

All the time Steve had been looking out of the window O'Donnell had sat completely unmoved and unmoving. His face was an expressionless mask. It was obvious he was in control here.

"Was it necessary for so many people to die?" Steve asked.

O'Donnell shrugged, his whole manner suggesting that he hadn't given the matter any thought, and even if he had it wouldn't have made any difference.

"They were in the wrong place at the wrong time. It happens. You must know that."

Steve inclined his head. He knew only too well that it did happen; there were some equations where the innocence of victims did not rate a high priority weighting.

"But what about the woman?" he asked.

"Ah, Leila. She was, let's say, beginning to be a cause

for concern to us," answered O'Donnell, without any emotion in his voice. There was a silence, but when it was obvious that there was to be no further gratuitous information coming, Steve persisted.

"So it was you who triggered the bomb." It was a statement, not a question.

"Why should that bother you?"

Steve didn't answer immediately but went back to leaning on the cabinet. He tried to assess his position. Whichever way he looked at it, it seemed anything but good.

"It may have escaped your notice, but I might have been one of those the police are trying to match arms and legs for," he said eventually in a low voice which mixed anger and sarcasm in equal measure.

"I had to see if your reflexes were still up to it, Steve. Time can catch up on all of us, you know. But if it will make you happier, I can tell you the device wasn't activated until you were just about to enter Via de Trebbio."

"Well now you know, and if you think I'm going to throw in my lot to work with you, you're..."

"Don't say it Steve," O'Donnell interrupted, "at least, not before you cast your eyes over these." He picked up a large envelope which had been lying on the floor to the left of his chair. From it he slid out half a dozen 10 by 6 black and white photographs and with exaggerated care placed them side by side on the cabinet. They were a sequence of shots of Steve calling the dog across to him, handling its collar, bending to examine it more closely and then the last, blurred where the others were sharp, showed him leaping over the wall.

Steve didn't really need to look at them, although he took his time to do so; he knew that he'd been well and truly stitched up.

"There is a video as well, of course," added O'Donnell.

"I wouldn't have expected less, but I hope you managed to get my best side," snarled Steve as he flicked through the stills.

"If you have one then we'll have it," answered O'Donnell.

Steve roughly gathered the photographs up and threw them down onto the floor in the general direction of the envelope. "So what's next?" he asked.

"To some extent that depends on others. But you probably don't need me to tell you that the Italian police don't take kindly to bombers," said O'Donnell. "And I'm pleased to say that these," he tapped a thick forefinger on the photographs before replacing them in the envelope, "and the video, are even better than I'd hoped. They show remarkably clearly that it was you who placed the device on the dog's neck." He spread his hands, in a gesture absolving himself of any involvement in the affair, and gave a cold smile. "I think you'll view all of this in a different light tomorrow," he added. "Macbride will be in touch then." He pushed himself onto his feet. "It may be that we won't meet again, in which case I'll say goodbye, Mr. Cromarty."

The meeting was at an end.

'Don't bank on us not meeting again', thought Steve as he left room 114 and made his way down the stairs to the reception lobby.

As he walked back to his new lodgings he passed Macbride's corner – as he'd expected; it was empty. So he'd have to be patient and wait for Macbride to contact him. On the other hand if he found he had time on his hands he did have a telephone number – Annie's. He decided that even that enticing prospect would have to wait until the morning; at the moment sleep seemed like a good idea.

★ ★ ★

From O'Donnell's point of view the meeting with Steve had gone as planned. However, alarm bells would have been ringing if he'd realised that the Roma was of so much interest to the security authorities that it was under general surveillance. On that particular day Nino Zavarelli had been assigned to the task. Of the various uniformed police forces in Italy, the *carabinieri* are held in the highest esteem.

But although their members are proud of their force's reputation, they are also very aware that a reputation alone doesn't put food on the table. For many of them, if they were given the choice of either pulling on the dark blue and black gear or having extra euros each month, the larger pay cheque would be an easy winner.

Nino Zavarelli had only been out of the uniform branch for a short time and he was ultra-keen to make a good impression. It was a trial period and he was uncomfortably aware of the many others who would leap at the chance of taking over from him if he didn't make the grade. "It's not just a question of keeping your nose clean," his superintendent had told him the first morning he had joined the squad. "I'll be looking for something positive." That had been five weeks ago. He knew that keenness by itself wouldn't be enough, but as yet he hadn't been presented with any sort of opportunity which would enable him to make a mark. And now Elena had told him she was pregnant again, so it was even more essential that he kept his position in security for the extra money it brought in.

It was this combination of personal circumstances that probably resulted in him being even more alert and vigilant than usual as he helped to man the reception desk of the Hotel Roma on the day Steve Cromarty arrived there. He hadn't actually booked him in - one of the bona fide clerks had done that – but he had taken notice of him, as he had of all the other guests. Then, later in the day after the explosion further down the street, he had been informed that the Englishman had moved out. This was surely too good to be true. Then, almost before his report on this was being read at headquarters, the man returned and asked him for directions to room 114; the room which was permanently booked out to Conquisto Film Corporation for entertainment purposes. The very reason he was there was that security believed it was a front for some sort of organisation run by Sean O'Donnell, and O'Donnell was the owner of the Irish Pub, where the explosion had occurred.

Zavarelli's second report set wheels in motion. As a direct result of this, from the moment Steve left the hotel at the conclusion of his meeting with O'Donnell, he was under team surveillance.

CHAPTER FIVE

Early morning in the Via del Moro was not exactly the quiet, peaceful time Steve had envisaged. Even though the apartment was well cushioned by the courtyard and the thick outer wall leading onto the street, the original builders couldn't have had modern traffic in mind. As a result there was a fairly continuous low-level hum, punctuated at intervals by the heavy growls of low-geared lorries. Like all major western cities, the servicing of the fruit and vegetable markets of Florence usually started somewhere between three and four in the morning.

As Steve struggled in vain to blot out the noise from his consciousness he wondered momentarily how Macbride was faring on his flagstones, which were only yards from the road; perhaps semi-oblivion by means of the bottle was making it bearable for him.

By shortly after six, Steve had reluctantly given up any hope of salvaging a further hour of sleep and he was up, showered and dressed. Not knowing what the day was going to throw at him, he couldn't have said with any confidence that he was ready for it. However, he knew that if the events of yesterday were anything to go by he had to do something in the way of preparation. It already seemed an age since he'd landed at Pisa Airport and yet less than twenty-four hours had passed. The business trip was not turning out at all as he'd thought and yet, in a strange way, he found himself pleased, even excited, at the situation he found himself in. It was probably the thought that he was back in with the things he'd been doing when he was twenty.

He pulled himself up short. He shouldn't be a bloody fool. Twenty was a long time back, even if some others tried to ignore the fact; you just had to think of Macbride, a tired-looking, paunchy has-been.

But the thought and the mental image of Macbride dragged him out of this negative reverie. Macbride was still in some way operational and he had probably been instrumental in pulling him back into the system; all right, he wouldn't have Steve's welfare at the top of his list of priorities, but when someone shows some level of confidence in you, you feel bound to give it a go. In that way he made the argument for his involvement. In any case he was very aware that if he needed further convincing, the evidence linking him to the bombing was the clincher.

He had no option. He was deeply involved, and somehow he had to make sure he was up to it. He had to get back into the bastard state of mind, he reminded himself as he started to make a search of the apartment.

It took him no more than twenty minutes. There was nothing of great interest; the place had been well furnished but sanitised. There was no sign of permanent occupancy; no magazines or papers lying around, no bathroom clutter. This didn't surprise him. It was a short-stay safe house, an upmarket bolt-hole.

After his initial tour of the place, he concentrated his attention on the kitchen. There were no knives that might suit his purpose, but one of the built-in wall cupboards held the electricity fuse box. As he had hoped, in a city where basic amenities were not always up to the standard in the UK, he found a card of spare fuse wire nicely to hand. The 15-amp wire was the one he wanted. He had always found this to be an annoyingly tedious task, but even though he did not know how much time he had before he might have a visitor, he had to force himself to be patient and not rush the job. If it wasn't done properly he might as well walk down the street with a placard around his neck announcing to all and sundry, "Look at my shoelaces, they've got wire threaded through them".

After ten minutes' careful work he was satisfied that the result would stand up to reasonable scrutiny. It was still only a few minutes after seven. There didn't seem much point in hanging around; there had been no suggestion from either O'Donnell or Macbride that he should keep off the streets, and he was sure Macbride would find him when he wanted to. He also felt it would be no bad thing to indicate to O'Donnell that he wasn't prepared to be completely in his pocket.

He decided to ring Annie. At this hour she would surely be at home, although she might not be over the moon at being woken up by a mid-forties 'twenty-year-old' looking for a female guide plus whatever extras might be thrown in. But she had given him her number, so she could hardly blame him for taking the opportunity.

Having decided that using the phone in the apartment would probably be the same as ringing O'Donnell direct, and as the only phone booth he was aware of was near the Irish Pub, he had no option other than to make his way past the bomb site. Workers had obviously been very busy during the night, as the scene of the devastation had been largely cleared. Only the jagged remains of the foundation of the demolished wall and several boarded-up windows and doors suggested that anything untoward had happened there.

The volume of traffic had now built up to a steady stream, but Steve was one of the few pedestrians. Two street cleaners in bright green coveralls slowly pushed long-handled brooms across the stone-floored, arched areas, depositing last night's debris of discarded papers and remains of fruit from the stalls into the steady flow of water which was running along the gutter. Not for the first time, Steve wondered how it was that so many foreign cities used this cleansing system, but not Britain.

Looking at the cleaners, who had now met at Macbride's corner and were having a rest and a chat, Steve saw that there was no sign of Macbride. Perhaps this was the time of day when he breakfasted while his living area was being spruced up, he mused; a far cry from the days of the au pairs which had been his normal diet.

In the phone booth he tapped out Annie's number. He let it ring for several minutes without being answered and then hung up. "Come on Annie, this is no way to treat a friend," he muttered before re-checking the number from the slip of paper she'd given him and then trying again. This time it was answered almost immediately – or at least the receiver was picked up. Steve waited a moment, thinking he was being connected to an answering machine, but there was nothing. The silence dragged on and was becoming to be something of an embarrassment, especially as one of the street cleaners had wandered that way and was beginning to take an interest. Reluctantly he felt obliged to make the first move.

"I think seeing the sights is more fun if two are playing, don't you?" he said.

"Don't build up your hopes, Steve."

It was Macbride's voice; deep, gravelly and yet refined – 'the real me', he'd once been heard to say before he'd sold his soul to the devil for the second time.

"What the hell are you doing there?" asked Steve, beginning to see the alluring prospect of a pleasant day in Florence rapidly disappearing. There was no way he'd wanted the contact with Macbride to be as soon as this.

"What I'm doing here is almost certainly what you'd like to be doing here," answered Macbride, with what Steve thought was a note of triumph in his voice. "You didn't honestly think I lived seven days a week on that street corner did you?"

"No, you always did find some other poor sod to do that," answered Steve bitterly.

"Now Steve, it's pointless being warped by what happened in the past, it's gone forever," said an unperturbed Macbride. "Here's Annie to entertain you. She's part of the future, so get into charm mode."

There was a moment's silence before Annie came on the line. "Hello Steve. Don't believe a word he says, it's just an old man dreaming."

Her voice was like a welcome breath of fresh air to Steve and, with its slight lilt, it seemed to come straight from the Rosslare of his youth.

"Are you the official entertainments girl?" he asked, trying to keep a note of disappointment from his tone.

"Sometimes it's necessary," she answered, "but with you I reckon it'll be no hardship."

"Well that's good to hear, but how do we take it further?" He shifted the receiver to his other ear and turned away from one of the cleaners, who was gesticulating at him through the glass.

"Listen carefully," she said. "At ten you must meet me at the west door of the Baptistry. Before then get yourself a duffle bag, nothing too flash, and a small automatic camera. Remember you are a tourist. Oh, and it's shirt sleeve order. It can get pretty hot where we'll be going." She rang off before Steve had time to put any further questions to her.

Pushing his way out of the phone booth, he had to step round the young street cleaner who had been trying to attract his attention and was waiting to sluice the pavement there.

"A bad night sir, a very bad thing," said the cleaner.

Steve was about to turn on him when he realised that he was referring to the previous night's explosion, not to the snippet of telephone conversation that he might have overheard.

"Si, si. Very bad." Steve shook his head to match the lad's sorrowful expression.

"I cannot clean and it is my pavement. Who could have done this to me?"

Steve looked at him in disbelief. Less than ten hours before young folk, much the same age as the cleaner, had been killed, maimed or disfigured and all he was concerned about was the damage to his cleaning area. Some inhabit a strange, narrow world, he thought.

"Make your point to the Commissioner of Police," he told the cleaner. "I'm sure he'll be delighted to hear your view." He clapped a consoling hand on the lad's shoulder, then left him trying to make sense of the remark and made his way back to the apartment. He too had a puzzle to consider, as it was Annie who had made the arrangement with him, not Macbride as O'Donnell had said.

Back in the apartment he rechecked his wallet, transferring only the essentials to money belt and trouser pockets until he could buy the duffle bag, and packed most of his non-essentials into the in-flight bag. The last thing he wanted to do was to leave too much in the apartment for others to paw over in his absence. He reckoned the station left luggage would take care of the bag and he would be able to find a place around there where he could have breakfast.

It was an easy walk to the station, across the square and alongside the old columned wall of the graveyard of the Santa Maria Novella church. At the first fast-food bar he came to, he dawdled over coffee and bread rolls. At that time in the morning the place wasn't exactly heaving with customers, so there was no one clearing the tables around him. From there, after depositing his bag, he went down to the underground shopping arcade, where he bought a mock-leather duffle bag and an Olympus Trip camera; not over the top in terms of price but one that he felt sure wouldn't disgrace him if he was ever seen dead with it. He was almost tempted by the bouquets of flowers in an adjoining stall, but decided that although Annie might be impressed, Macbride certainly wouldn't be.

Back on street level, a fifteen-minute stroll brought him to within sight of the Baptistry. Early tourists, fresh from their breakfasts in their rooms, were already five or six deep admiring the panelled doors and trying to agree on whether it was the north door or the east door they were looking at before frantically thumbing through their guide books.

"This one's just a copy, George," said a blonde Monroe lookalike.

"Okay honey, let's not waste our time."

Steve didn't have a guide book, so for him it was a quick glance and then into the Baptistry itself. There, by means of some inconsiderate pushing, he managed to wedge himself into a corner and let the crowds spill past him. The Baptistry was a place where good livings were made. In the course of the next half hour he saw eight purses lifted, and he reckoned that there were probably double that which he didn't see. With all eyes directed up to the renowned ceiling, the men feeling secure with their money belts and their wives holding the necessary cash for the day and close bodily contact unavoidable, it could almost be the ultimate realisation of the proverbial manna from heaven.

He watched, not without some grudging admiration of the pickpockets' skill, but he took no action; he didn't see it as his place to become involved in other people's economics. In any case, after the initial shock, it would provide a further talking point for them when they returned home and were regaling friends about the perils of Europe.

When it was almost ten o'clock he allowed himself to be shuffled out with the next exiting group and found himself blinking in the bright sunshine. Already the temperature was creeping into the mid-twenties – Annie had been right about the need for shirt sleeve order.

"Right on time." It was Annie, linking her arm into his. "I see you've done your shopping," she added, indicating the bag he had on one shoulder. "What sort of camera did you get?"

Steve showed her the Olympus, which she examined with what seemed to be real interest. He was pleased to see she approved of his purchase but, for a reason he couldn't fathom, he felt a little concerned that already that should be important to him.

"But fancy," Annie continued, "all those flower shops and you never thought to buy me any."

"I thought," countered Steve. "But then I also wondered how Macbride would react. I wouldn't want to queer his pitch."

Annie stopped in her tracks and turned square on to him, oblivious to a group of complaining pedestrians who were forced to step around her.

"We're all sorry for Macbride," she said quietly. "Anybody would be. But he's just a pathetic, washed-out old man. Surely you didn't think…" She gave an exaggerated shudder.

Steve didn't go along with Annie's assessment – Macbride was no spent force - but he wasn't going to argue the point. They continued walking back the way Steve had come earlier, but this time Annie was guiding the way, her arm still in his. At the first flower shop Steve pulled her inside and bought a single green and white orchid in a cellophane box. Outside the shop, Annie kissed him.

"Do you know, deep down, I think you're a romantic sort of guy," she said.

"Sorry to disillusion you, but I'm an out-and-out opportunist." He smiled at her, stroked his hand down her back and lightly smacked her bottom.

Within a few minutes they had reached the Piazza della Stazione, which was now a roaring four-lane mass of vehicles. Annie took them past the entrance to the underpass which was there for the faint-hearted who were not prepared to run the gauntlet of make-believe F1 drivers. Instead she turned into the Via Caterina da Siena and then into the SITA bus station. It was empty of both prospective passengers and buses. At the counter she bought one return ticket to San Gimignano. They then sat on the hard, plastic seats in the draughty concourse where the only other life was a couple of dowdy pigeons picking at scraps among cigarette debris.

"Why aren't you coming?" asked Steve.

"Don't worry, I am," she replied. "I'll join you at a place called Poggibonsi. It'll take the bus about an hour to get there and it's a scheduled ten-minute halt. I'll watch you get on here in case you're being followed, then I'll travel by car. If for some reason I don't meet up with you then you'll just have to be a lone tourist for the day and I'll see you back here off the six o'clock return bus."

Other people now arrived, obviously more au fait with the timetable, as the bus slowly nosed its way into the bay. Annie held Steve back while the other passengers pushed and shoved each other to get on, even though it was patently obvious that there was more than enough room for all of them. "Mussolini got the trains and buses to run on time," muttered Steve. "If he could have got the people to adopt the discipline to form queues they might have won the war."

"Before my time, darling," said Annie, giving him another quick kiss on the cheek. Then, waving the boxed orchid in front of her like a banner, she hurried out of the station, leaving Steve admiring her style but wondering how carefully she was watching for possible tails.

CHAPTER SIX

As soon as the last of his jostling fellow travellers had boarded, Steve joined them. He casually waved his ticket at the driver, who indicated the validation machine, then shrugged his shoulders at him. There were several vacant seats, but he chose one beside the window, near the back, on the offside of the vehicle.

Once settled, he decided that he had three possible ways of spending the hour until Poggibonsi was reached where, he hoped, Annie would rejoin him. First he could observe his fellow passengers. He did this for all of ten minutes and came to the conclusion that a small number of them were tourists and were either the same Americans and Japanese he'd seen last night or very close relatives of them. The rest were elderly Italians, men and women, some with young grandchildren with them, who only travelled for two or three stops before being replaced by others.

The second possibility was to look at the countryside.

As he hadn't travelled any distance on buses for years, he'd forgotten how their routes passed through small towns and villages as well as countryside, whereas railways always seem to snake their way through industrial zones and around the backs of unkempt blocks of flats with grubby washing hanging listlessly in search of a breeze. However, after a quarter of an hour of admiring warm, red-tiled villas with gardens filled with blossoming shrubs and the dark, geometrical lines of poplars on Apennine foothills, he felt the Tuscan message had got through to him loud and clear.

The third possibility was to try to sort out in his mind just what he had become involved in. Where did Macbride and Annie fit into it? Where was Annie now? Despite her claim, he was sure that she hadn't checked out any of the other passengers. Would O'Donnell carry out his threat of informing the police if he decided to give the whole thing the heave-ho? As yet he had no answer to any of these questions, but he felt the risk of calling O'Donnell's bluff was too high, so he would just have to go along with things at least for a while.

He began to look for signposts. At the next crossroads there was a board which read 'Poggibonsi 8'. He hoped Annie would join him there – not only would the day turn horribly flat if she didn't, but there'd be no chance of prising any information from her, and he was badly in need of some.

A few minutes later the bus pulled in beside a nondescript, single-storey building which looked as though it might originally have been painted white and then rendered with a thin coat of light grey-green dust. However, it wasn't just a stop; it was the transfer point Annie had mentioned.

The driver got out, lit a cigarette, then strolled across the road and disappeared into a rest area. Then three Italian couples got on, elderly like the others, but without imitating a rugby scrum as they did so. An old dog and a cat lay together, taking advantage of the shade provided by a low, wooden seat. It was that sort of place; tired, sleepy in the heat, even the air seemed reluctant to stir. And this was probably its busiest time, thought Steve.

Of far more importance to him, he could see no sign of Annie. Did that mean there had been a tail placed on his movements? Only the tourists on the bus showed any signs of impatience; the elderly Italians simply carried on with their conversations or sat staring idly, unconcernedly, out of the windows at the dusty street scene.

Eventually the driver reappeared and without showing the least sign of urgency, made his way back to his bus. He glanced both ways up the road as if expecting late arrivals to suddenly appear, and then with great deliberation he hitched up his trousers and hauled himself up into his cab. He had started the engine and was noisily engaging first gear when Annie suddenly plonked herself onto the seat beside Steve.

"Were you thinking I hadn't made it?" she laughed. "Don't look so amazed. I got Giorgio, the driver, to open the back door for me." Steve smiled with her, mainly to hide his annoyance. But it was really much more than annoyance; he was appalled with himself – he was still not into automatic mode.

"I think we're going to have a good day, I can feel it in my bones," said Annie. "I'm sure you're going to love the place."

"You're probably right, but it's more likely if you'll just fill me in with some details about this whole set-up."

"Steve, I honestly don't know and I don't ask. Believe me. In any case Macbride will be seeing you tonight, so you can ask him." She turned and gazed out of the window for a time before continuing. "Isn't this a fabulous road? The first time I travelled on it I was on the back of a scooter driven by…"

Steve put the fingers of his left hand over her lips and stopped her from completing the sentence.

"I've known some women who use talk as a substitute for sex," he said. "Not all the time, just when they couldn't get it."

"So women talk to you a lot, is that what you're saying?" She looked at him with an expression which suggested experience well beyond her twenty-odd years. That look jolted Steve's memory. A view of the world according to McKenna – for information or help in a strange city, where do bastards go? To the dropouts who live on the streets and the girls who work on the streets. The girls in particular were generally more lucid and could usually offer a service far more comprehensive than the average client would dream of. Steve could still remember the times when he had been thankful for that.

It came back to him now what Annie had said when he had first met her – she'd said that she only worked two days a week at the Irish pub and she'd made no reference as to how she filled in her time on the other five days.

"You don't really believe that," he said in answer to her question. "Now let's just enjoy our day." He dropped his hand onto her thigh and gently squeezed.

The road twisted and turned as it wound its way up the hillside, with the driver relying on frequent use of the two-tone horn to warn oncoming traffic and hopefully ensure the blind corners were clear for him. As the drops visible from the bus windows became more and more precipitous, Steve realised why the driver had made such a play of hitching up his trousers. If he'd only bothered to tell us, we could all have hitched up, he thought; it might have helped.

Safely at the top of the climb, all the passengers alighted

with what seemed like a collective sigh of relief. Annie held Steve back for a few minutes while the rest moved away. "We don't want to be part of a gawping gaggle," she said. "It'll spoil the atmosphere of the place."

Hand in hand, they strolled across the gravelled and grassed area to the south gateway, the Porta San Giovanni, and through its arched entrance into the medieval town. Steve did not consider himself to be utterly cultureless, although even on one of his better days he reckoned he would only have been welcome in the Philistines' second team, but here even he couldn't help but be impressed.

"Well? What do you think of it?" asked Annie, after they'd walked part way up the narrow, cobbled main street.

He nodded his appreciation. "I think we'd better not breathe too deeply or we'll end up in the 1500s or whenever," he said. He pulled the camera out of its case. "Now let's play the tourists. Stand over there."

For the next hour they wandered, enjoying both the place and each other's company. Along with the hundreds of others who were there, Steve found himself taking photographs at almost every corner they turned as towers, palaces, cloisters and courtyards demanded to be captured on film.

"We'll have lunch in the Bar le Torri in the cathedral square", said Annie. "They know me so we'll get a table. Then after that I want you to take my photo alongside the well in the Piazza della Cisterna. It's just down from here."

"We can go and take it now, before we have lunch – there's time," he said.

"No," she insisted. "This is where local knowledge comes in useful. At about three o'clock the sun is just right to light up the stonework. It'll be perfect then."

"Okay, you're the guide."

So they had lunch first at a table which was made available for them as soon as one of the waiters spotted Annie coming into the bar. The meal, selected mainly by Annie with minimal input from Steve, was excellent – *prosciutto e fiche verdi* followed by *bistecca alla brace e patatine arroste*, then *torta alle mandorle,* accompanied by a Chianti Classico Riserva. They ate at a pace which allowed them to fully appreciate it.

It wasn't until they were back in the square at three o'clock that Steve was made to realise the significance of these delaying tactics by Annie. He had just lined her up for a photograph with the greyish-white travertine stone standing out against the russet brickwork of the surrounding medieval buildings when she suddenly jumped towards him.

"Let's get someone to take the two of us together," she said. "I'll get somebody." She unhooked the camera strap from around his neck. "You stand by the well to keep the place."

He did so, much to the annoyance of a large group of Asian visitors, and then Annie ran back and jammed herself against him. "Smile!" she whispered as the young, slim Italian she'd got to take the photograph bent over the camera. The camera clicked and the man straightened up. Annie hurried back to him, pushing her way through the crowd, to retrieve the camera.

No words were spoken and the Italian turned and was immediately lost in the crowd, but from the brief glimpse Steve had got of him he would have been prepared to bet money that it was Lorenzo, O'Donnell's minder.

Steve took the camera from Annie and put it back into its case. They then started to make their way back to the Porta San Giovanni, this time taking the slightly less crowded Via Berignano. They didn't speak for a while. Then Steve gently eased her into a doorway, casually put his arm around her neck and bent his head down to her face. To all the world it looked as if they were simply kissing.

"It's not the same camera," he whispered to her, "and it was Lorenzo who took the photograph of us back there."

It was a shot in the dark, but as Annie made no attempt to deny it or bluster it out he knew he was right. With just a little more arm pressure, making her wince, he added, "Don't ever set me up again without letting me know in advance." Then he kissed her.

An awkward silence hung between them on the return journey to Florence. Steve eventually broke it.

"I know you've already said that you don't know much about what you've got yourself into. And I suppose that's your business. But tell me about the camera switch. Why?"

Annie turned and looked closely at him. She was obviously in a dilemma. How much did he need to know? How much should she tell him?

"That was Lorenzo's idea," she said finally. "He thought it would be better if what O'Donnell wants us to carry was taken on by you, at least for a while."

"And O'Donnell doesn't know." It was a statement, not a question. Annie simply nodded and Steve left it at that. The trip hadn't been wasted – he had a potential bargaining counter.

CHAPTER SEVEN

Back in the Florence apartment, Steve had a shower, helped himself to a beer from the fridge, then settled down to wait for callers. Annie had left him when the bus reached the outskirts of the city, saying she had various bits of shopping to do but she would catch up with him later. He had been quite happy with that arrangement, as it gave him time alone in the apartment to check out the camera more closely. As he'd expected, it was the same make and model as the one he'd bought that morning. He recalled how keen Annie had been to examine it closely before she'd left him to travel to Poggibonsi on his own.

He decided not to open it, but wrapped it in a polythene bag from the kitchen and found a temporary lodging place for it, sitting snugly under a geranium in a window box two doors down the street. He now knew for sure that the camera had been switched in San Gimignano. But why had they gone to the bother? Annie had obviously not gone with him for the first part of the bus journey, not, as she had said, to watch for possible tails but to inform Lorenzo of the make of camera so he could make the switch. But where could O'Donnell and Macbride fit into this? Surely O'Donnell had to be involved because he was going to put money up front; although as yet he hadn't done so, Steve reminded himself. As for Macbride who, according to O'Donnell, should be contacting him today but hadn't yet done so, what role did he have? Steve couldn't come up with an answer.

After a fruitless hour of waiting he felt tempted to go along to the square to see if Macbride was still in residence, but he thought better of it. After all someone might call while he was away – Annie, for instance. She had promised to make things up to him, and even though he now had more than passing doubts about her motives, he was quite prepared to let her run through her physical repertoire. Another possibility was that someone from O'Donnell might arrive to talk money and, again, he would rather not miss that.

He was about to open a second beer when the telephone rang. The noise was shrill and in the otherwise silent room it was insistent, but he waited, resisting the urge to grab at it. He was beginning to feel a little vulnerable; all the more reason to take things slowly.

He opened the second beer, took a long swig from the

bottle and settled himself in the easy chair on the opposite side of the room from the telephone. Perhaps it wasn't for him; in fact it almost certainly wasn't, he thought, as only three people knew he was there and he didn't expect telephones to be their message carriers. It could ring on until whoever it was got tired.

Just as he'd decided on this course of inaction, the apartment door was pushed open and Annie rushed in, almost tripping over her large shopping bag as she grabbed the receiver.

"Hello? Oh Jason. No, I've just this minute got in. What? Oh yes, I sometimes leave a light on. No, I can't tonight. Girlfriends, yes. Ring me tomorrow."

She rang off and turned to face Steve, a frown on her face.

"If I'm being something of an inconvenience…" he said and then just let his voice trail away.

She shook her head. "Far from it, but I'm pleased you didn't answer that."

"I take it you'd rather not have a jealous Jason on your hands," he teased.

"No, it's nothing like that. Believe me." The worried look was still on her face.

"Then what?"

"Jason is not always the most discreet," she answered. "If he'd heard your voice it's more than likely that half of

Florence would know you were here by tomorrow morning and that wouldn't be in the interests of any of us."

"So why do you mix with him?"

"As far as possible I don't. But some business associates of Mr O'Donnell think he's rather nice – the current flavour of the month." She twisted her mouth to indicate her disgust. "The big trouble will come when he falls from favour. Anyone who says that thing about a woman scorned hasn't met the Jasons of this world."

Steve felt a ripple of unease run across the small of his back. He reflected that if there was going to be any trouble, he would be better off with Macbride standing there in place of Annie. Macbride might be considered by some to be old and paunchy, 'pathetic and washed out', hadn't Annie said, but at that moment he just seemed to have a bit more to offer than a five feet four, eight stone, twentyish female, no matter if she would measure eight point five on a Richter beauty scale.

One other thing Annie had was the contents of the shopping bag, which she started to unpack onto the small coffee table beside Steve's chair.

"I think you'll be most interested in this. It's from Mr O'Donnell," she said.

So she had obviously had time to scuttle back to him.

Steve drew a bulky manila envelope across and examined it. It was the sort of envelope that could be bought at any cheap stationery store worldwide for something under a penny each, or the local equivalent. "He's not afraid of pushing the boat out," Steve muttered sarcastically. But as he ripped open the top, he gave a low whistle. The noise stopped Annie pulling out the rest of the bag's contents, which seemed to be mainly in the food line. She looked across at him.

"Seems as though I was doing him a bit of an injustice," continued Steve as he extracted a large wad of hundred-euro notes and fanned them with his thumb. "Looks more than promising, don't you think?"

"He's only buying you like he tries to buy everybody," said Annie, in a tone which suggested that O'Donnell and contempt were interchangeable in her book.

"Everything has its price in the real world, Annie," he retorted. "Even you."

"No, that's not true." Her eyes were suddenly fiercely lit and focused on him. "Don't think for a minute that I do what I do for the money."

"Don't tell me you're one of those principled women who only fuck for a cause."

It was then she hit him – a sharp, backhanded blow whose force came not from the shoulder but from the forearm and the hard edge of her open hand caught Steve high up on his left cheek. A few millimetres to the right and he knew he would have been looking down a broken nose. As he blinked away the tears that had appeared in the corners of his eyes he had the distinct impression that it hadn't been his luck which had saved his features. In that moment he reassessed her. This was a girl he had to get to know better.

"Okay, so that's sorted," he said, gingerly running his fingers over his cheek. "Any other finer feelings I should stay clear of?"

Annie smiled and reached across to touch his hand. "Given time I think we could get to understand each other. But I'm afraid we might not have the time."

"Why?" Steve asked, hoping he hadn't just imagined a wistful tone in her voice.

"Macbride should be here in the next few minutes," she said. "With him around I don't know if we'll be able to indulge in anything other than business."

Steve said nothing. He watched her transferring the food into the fridge in the kitchen and then went back into the living room to take a quick glance at himself in the mirror above the empty fireplace. His cheek felt very tender, but he was relieved to see the skin wasn't broken. Although the bruising would show later, it shouldn't be necessary to come up with an explanation to Macbride tonight.

He was about to go back into the kitchen when he heard a loud scuffling in the outer patio area. It only lasted seconds, and then the door opened and a young man was almost thrown bodily into the room, coming to a halt on his hands and knees at Steve's feet. He was followed, at a much more leisurely pace, by Macbride, who was dusting his hands together as though he felt it necessary to rid himself of some sort of contamination.

Annie, aware of the commotion, had come out of the kitchen and now all three of them were standing looking down at a young black man who appeared to be terrified out of his wits.

It was Annie who spoke first. "Jason, you fool!"

"So this one's Jason, is it?" said Macbride, giving the man a non-too-gentle poke in the ribs with the toe of his shoe. From the wince of pain it seemed Jason already had a couple of broken ribs, at the very least. That didn't surprise Steve. He knew from way back that Macbride was a firm believer in the view that rib damage will bring anyone low, no matter how big they are. The opposing view that groins or kneecaps were more effective he'd always dismissed as too low a percentage choice – too difficult to hit effectively and you don't always get a second chance.

"I think I should talk to him later, Annie," continued Macbride, "but we need to go out for our chat first." He nodded his head towards Steve as he spoke. "In the meantime keep him here for me, secure."

Annie went back into the kitchen and within a few

minutes returned with a hessian sack and a rope clothes line. Jason, who didn't really seem to know what was going on, allowed her to pull him up into a sitting position. She flung the sack over his head and shoulders and tied the rope around his chest and upper arms, pulling it tight until he gave another yelp of pain. Then she thrust him unceremoniously back onto the floor.

Steve and Macbride watched in silence and nodded approval of her professionalism.

"You just never know when that particular Brownie's badge will come in useful, do you?" commented Steve.

Macbride inclined his head towards Steve and spoke quietly out of the corner of his mouth.

"More like bondage work to me," he said. Then, straightening up, he indicated that it was time for the two of them to leave. "We'll be about an hour or just over," he said to Annie.

Without waiting for a reply, he led Steve back through the outer area and into the street.

CHAPTER EIGHT

There were few people out, and those who were were not loitering, as there was now a stiff breeze funnelling up from the direction of the Arno. The sky above the narrow streets was turning into an angry, ominous purple–grey.

"The sort of night to suit our purpose," said Macbride. He led the way towards the river and then took them over it by the Ponte alla Carrala. At the far side he cut through a narrow alley which turned sharp right at the end to face an area of waste ground. They made their way across this. The huge bulk of the Pitti Palace loomed ahead, but their destination proved to be somewhat less grand. Almost at the boundary of the waste ground, where some partially-scrubbed-up bushes were somehow surviving, stood an old, wooden shed, presumably left behind when the demolition men had moved on. It looked as though it would be fortunate to see out another storm.

Macbride half-pushed and half-lifted open the rickety

door. Inside there were several packing cases, some covered with filthy, torn sheets of polythene, and dozens of empty cans and bottles. Steve took his cue from Macbride and seated himself on one of the cases.

"I know it's not the most salubrious of meeting places," said Macbride, airily waving an arm around at the squalor, "but at least it's safe."

"Are you telling me the apartment isn't safe?" Steve asked.

Macbride gave him an old, tired look and shrugged his heavy shoulders before replying. "Not for us, Steve. We're in a situation of running with at least two packs. And if you cast your mind back you'll remember that always brings complications."

Steve gave a sigh and pursed his lips. "Why are you never involved with things which are simple? And why pull me into it?"

"Simple things, as you well know, don't tax my intelligence sufficiently." He gave a self-deprecating smile and waited a moment before continuing. "And you also know that's bollocks – the truth is they tend not to pay well enough."

As Steve looked at Macbride he was aware of a welter of emotions. This was a man he had good cause to hate, but he also knew that in spite of that there was a bond between them, a special relationship, one forged by shared dangers.

"You want to know, why you," continued Macbride. "Because you were the only one well cooled enough and available. And I agreed to have you," he added, almost as a grudging afterthought.

"You didn't bring me to this shack so I could thank you for getting me a job," answered Steve impatiently. "So just put me in the picture, eh?"

"Take your time, Steve. Rushing at it won't help," said Macbride, pulling a bottle from the inner pocket of his duffel-type coat. "Let's get ourselves settled first."

He took a long swig, then held the bottle across. Steve pushed it away; previous experience had taught him that he could match Macbride in many things, but drinking certainly wasn't one of them.

"Please yourself," Macbride said before taking another drink. He wiped the back of his hand across his lips before continuing.

"Where to start is always a problem. Perhaps with Mr Sean O'Donnell is the best place. You've already met him, a man who makes things happen. He's powerful, and don't ever forget that."

The first distant rumble of thunder seemed to underline the point Macbride was making.

"He's in more pies than any blackbird ever was." He took another swig from the bottle, and again Steve refused the offer to join him. "If he sang, the suicide rate would make it look like an epidemic had struck. And not just in Italy."

"How come?" Steve's question was almost drowned by another burst of thunder, nearer this time, and the walls of the shed seemed to give with the blast.

"Among other things, he feeds appetites. You've seen the young men, all of them smartly dressed, all available." The last word came out as a sneer before he took another drink. "But don't get the wrong idea about him. He's not your normal pimp. For him it's all insurance. It gives him power in the highest places so he can operate."

He shifted his bulk on the packing case, seeking a more comfortable position, and waited for a response from his guest. Steve also waited. O'Donnell's insurance methods weren't to his taste, but how and what he was operating would affect him, and he wanted information on that. And how did Macbride fit into all of this?

Eventually Macbride continued. "O'Donnell is a dealer in arms, drugs and anything else which is required by individuals or countries or organizations which will pay the highest prices, ask no questions, but expect the best. Until the peace process got under way in Northern Ireland there were arms shipments out by way of Genoa and then drug runs ending up in remote sea lochs in Scotland. We got two of those runs stopped."

"We?" queried Steve.

"Yes, we. During the time you were holed up I was infiltrated into O'Donnell's network and, would you believe it, he now trusts me. But he doesn't know who's looking after my pension fund, or yours for that matter, if you come up with the goods."

"Does the goods mean what is in the camera that was foisted on me?"

"Might be, but somehow I doubt it," answered Macbride. "But Lorenzo has got it into his head that it is, and he thinks he's going to make a killing with it, if you'll excuse the pun."

"So trusty minder Lorenzo thinks he's seen his big chance. Is that it?"

"He and Annie. But they've made a big mistake. O'Donnell suspects, and that's why you've been brought in. To help flush them out."

"It must be something hellish big that's involved for them to take the risk."

"Extra special doesn't cover it, Steve. Lorenzo's no fool. Somehow he knows what O'Donnell's got hold of and he's prepared to risk everything. What he doesn't know is that O'Donnell is just waiting to net him."

"And what is this extra special commodity, if it's not arms or drugs?"

"At the moment I, or I should say we, don't know," answered Macbride.

"But big enough to tempt Lorenzo to chance his arm," said Steve, "and for O'Donnell to keep close tabs on him."

"Exactly that."

"And big enough for you to pull me in?"

"He wanted the best, and you know what I think of you, so it was no contest."

"But he wanted proof, and the carnage outside the pub supplied that. Was that it?"

"Not my doing. My hands are clean." Macbride shrugged his shoulders. "But don't think I was happy with it. Leila and I had had some good times together in the past."

"And you reckon Annie's in with Lorenzo on this?"

"O'Donnell seems to think so."

"All very interesting," said Steve, "but how exactly am I to be fitted into this?"

"O'Donnell said he wanted a reliable runner, so our lords and masters thought of you. You and they will be driving back to your roots, supposedly as tourists." He pulled a large envelope out of his bottle pocket and handed it over. "Here's your itinerary and ferry tickets, courtesy of Sean O'Donnell. I believe you've already got your first payment from him."

Steve nodded and pocketed the envelope without opening it.

"Couldn't be more easily earned," added Macbride.

"Don't expect me to believe that. Remember you've

only hinted at an Irish pack," Steve reminded him. "What about others?"

"That's not so easily answered. The French are habitually worried and if they know you're travelling through they'll find a reason to have some involvement." He paused as another burst of thunder crashed almost directly overhead. "The Spanish are extremely edgy about the Basque truce, and they're also concerned about security in their North African enclaves. What you are carrying and its eventual destination will certainly be of interest to them."

"And I assume the British aren't completely disinterested in shafting O'Donnell," said Steve.

Macbride gave one of his rare smiles. "Yes I think you can safely assume that."

"In which case there should be another envelope of cash from them."

"Steve, whatever happened to your idealism?" answered Macbride, throwing out his arms in mock horror.

"My idealism, such as it was, vanished when you made no attempt to spring me from Buta. Remember?"

Macbride either chose to ignore the bitterness in Steve's tone or didn't hear it as the next rumble of thunder rolled and reverberated above them. "There were a lot of things happening then and priorities changed," he eventually answered. He took another swig from the bottle, made as if to offer it to Steve, then changed his mind, corked it and returned it to his pocket.

"Sod off. My priorities didn't change," replied Steve.

"Okay. You were left in the shit, but don't think I didn't feel for you. This time you'll get a nicely framed vellum certificate, posthumous of course, or 500,000 cash, if you're still in a fit state to squander it."

"And for that I suppose I have to trust you?"

"'Twas ever thus Steve," said O'Donnell, clapping him on the shoulder. "You'll be contacted. In the meantime follow O'Donnell's instructions to the letter. Now let's get back and remind young Jason that there are some things that are well beyond his reach."

He pulled open the door and they made their way back across the waste ground. The air was heavy, warm and sultry. Just as they reached the shelter of the first buildings, the black sky was cut by vivid electric-white flashes and the rolling thunder brought with it torrential rain that hurt the skin. Macbride broke into a run, and Steve was surprised at the effort he had to make to keep pace with him. He was pleased it was no more than a hundred yards before Macbride turned into a narrow side street and then stopped to take advantage of the shelter provided by a porticoed doorway.

"You see why Florence suits me," grinned Macbride, his thin hair plastered over a pale scalp and rainwater trickling down the deep furrows on both of his cheeks. "Because it's unpredictable, like me."

"Don't bother me with your self-analysis," answered Steve. "In any case you've got it wrong. You are predictable, just bloody unprincipled and undependable."

For a split second it looked as though Macbride was going to respond, but then, seeming to think better of it, he grunted, "Let's go."

Although the rain had hardly slackened, he set off, thrusting his head forward as if challenging the elements to do their worst. Steve followed , wondering if he had really touched a raw nerve, then as quickly rejecting the thought; Macbride's nerves had long since been cauterised.

Ten minutes later they were back in the Via del Moro. As they passed the place where Steve had deposited the camera, he hoped the rain hadn't washed the covering soil away, but there was no opportunity to check without Macbride seeing.

Macbride opened the street door to number 11 and they both passed through, pleased to be out of the storm. The interior courtyard area, sheltered as it was by the surrounding high buildings, was almost dry, making a mockery of their sodden coats. The interior door leading to the living quarters was locked, which Macbride had obviously not expected, as he had to search through several of his pockets, cursing softly to himself, before he found the key.

As he was searching, Steve had just the vaguest of

feelings that things weren't quite as they should have been. Perhaps it was the silence of the house; the lights were on, but not a living sound came from it. Or perhaps it was just the contrast of the stillness of the courtyard with the storm which they had just experienced and which was still raging over the city. Maybe, but the feeling persisted as he waited for Macbride to turn the four-barrel latch and push the door open.

"Annie, we're back!" Macbride's voice rang round the room.

"Jesus!" They both spoke together as they took in the scene. Only the heavy, mahogany sideboard appeared to be where it had been when they'd left the room just over an hour earlier. The rest of the furniture looked as if it had got in the way of over-enthusiastic bailiffs.

"Annie?" Macbride called again. He and Steve slowly and carefully began to make their way round the smashed coffee table and upturned armchairs. The settee was still upright but it had been dragged across the room so that it was now virtually blocking the doorway into the kitchen. It was the end nearest to Steve that provided the easiest route, and as he moved round it he saw the body. It was lying face up with a mass of semi-congealed blood on the chest.

Macbride, looking over Steve's shoulder, muttered an inaudible curse, then in a harsh whisper said, "This we could have done without."

"So could he, I guess," answered Steve. "And where's Annie?"

At that moment the kitchen door started to slowly open and there stood Annie, her red hair even redder against the whiteness of her face. In her left hand she held a long, sharp-pointed kitchen knife.

If Macbride felt any emotion he didn't show it – this Steve expected of him. But whereas once he would have looked on this as real professionalism he now, more than a decade out of touch with it, saw it as callousness; the man had been dehumanised by years of repressed feelings. This was the world he'd been dragged back into, and he knew that if he didn't match up then his chances of scooping first prize in the Irish National Lottery wouldn't be a great deal better than poor old Jason's.

"I take it we were mistaken when we thought you had got your knots badge in the Brownies," Macbride said, easing himself past Steve and calmly taking the knife from Annie. She made no protest. but just stared straight ahead. Macbride held her by the right elbow and then, when Steve had pulled the settee slightly away from the door, he led her round to it and sat her down. It was then that she dropped her head and started to talk rapidly.

"Shortly after you'd gone I went into the kitchen and made myself a coffee. I came back in here and he was waiting for me. I pulled the chairs and table between us

and told him to come to his senses. But he was mad. Mad!"
she repeated. "I could see that. I ran back into the kitchen,
but before I could shut the door against him he was there.
I grabbed the knife."

She stopped speaking, took a large gulp of air,
shuddered and ran her fingers through her hair. She then
looked straight at Steve before she continued.

"He pulled me back into here and dragged me down
behind this" – she tapped the arm of the settee - "and that's
when I used the knife."

Again she shuddered, putting her hands to the sides of
her head. Macbride took charge, which Steve was more
than happy with; after all, he reasoned, although Jason had
met his end in what was his temporary residence, Macbride
was the one with a permanent pad in fair Florence, even if
it was only a street corner.

"I'll take Annie back with me," he said to Steve, "and
don't worry about him." He nodded in the general
direction behind the settee. "I'll have him moved in the
morning. In the meantime, have a good·night. I think
you'll find you're leaving us tomorrow afternoon."

They left and Steve bolted the door, then surveyed the
scene of the wrecked living room while he considered what
to do next. He pulled one of the armchairs into its original
position and, as he did so, he saw the hessian sack which
Annie had placed over Jason's head and chest. He was about

to leave it where it was when he noticed the bloodstain on it. Picking it up and holding it up to the light, he saw that the slit through the sack was right in the centre of the bloodstain. At a rough guess, it would have been halfway down Jason's chest when it had been over him.

Steve sat down in the armchair. He felt tired and was ready for sleep, but he knew there were several things that needed to be done. The first, to retrieve the camera, only took him a few minutes. The second, checking the journey details, was also soon done – it was as Macbride had said, with a car available for him, ready fuelled, at 2 pm the following day being the start of it.

The third took a little longer. It was a long shot, but he couldn't entirely rid himself of the feeling that Macbride might be working to his own agenda, in which case he might need some sort of back-up.

He fell asleep in the chair without having resolved the fourth: why had Annie killed Jason in cold blood, and why had Macbride believed her story?

CHAPTER NINE

The night Annie had murdered Jason in the apartment in Florence would remain forever in her memory; it was the first time she had killed, but she was convinced she had had to do it.

Five minutes after Steve and Macbride had left, Jason had started shouting to be freed. She had ignored him until he made the crucial error of saying he would tell O'Donnell that she and Lorenzo were planning something. She grabbed the knife in the kitchen, only meaning to threaten him, but he wouldn't shut up so she stabbed him, once only, in the chest. Then, before Steve and Macbride returned, she dragged the furniture around, took the sack and rope off Jason's body and then carefully rehearsed her explanation. Strangely, she was more concerned about the risk she had to take after she'd allowed Macbride to take her back to her flat.

She forced herself to wait a full fifteen minutes to allow

him to get clear of the area before she set off for Lorenzo's place. Those minutes were awful. Trying to forget what had happened with Jason was not made any easier by thinking of what might lie ahead. She was very conscious of the fact that Lorenzo had been most reluctant to give her his address, and she had never been there before. Visiting him at this time of night, unannounced and uninvited, was an invasion she would rather have avoided. There was the distinct possibility that he would be drinking, or maybe even worse.

That sudden thought made her flesh creep and almost caused her to abandon the visit. But what else could she do? Lorenzo must be told, and she would have to take whatever his unpredictable temper might throw at her.

She paid off the taxi in the Via Favallia and walked the rest of the way. At least, she thought, he couldn't accuse her of being an unthinking, panicky female. The storm, which was still flickering around the city, had cleared people from the streets and fortunately she met no one, either in the entrance hallway of the block of flats or on the stairs up to his apartment.

When she pressed the doorbell it seemed to her that the sound filled and echoed down the corridor, and she willed Lorenzo to answer it quickly before any of the other second-floor occupants had felt obliged to investigate. Minutes passed and she began to fear that Lorenzo was spending the night elsewhere. She was about to ring again when the door was opened, but only as far as a short, but heavier than standard, chain would allow. Lorenzo looked at her through blurred, heavy-lidded eyes; he had been drinking and it took a moment for him to focus on her and realise who it was. He clumsily released the chain and then, with a muttered curse, he grabbed her arm, pulled her violently into the room and closed the door.

"You stupid, stupid fool of a bitch, what are you doing here?" he snarled at her. "I told you, you never come here. Never, you understand?"

Annie kept her head; she'd expected this sort of reception. At least there was no one else there to cause complications or to make Lorenzo feel he had to humiliate her.

"There was no other choice, Lorenzo."

"What?" His voice was high pitched and incredulous. "No other choice? No other choice than maybe destroy all our plans? Maybe even destroy us. Or is that what you're after?"

Suspicion swept across his clouded eyes. "Have you devised some sort of devious plan in that tiny Irish head of yours? Well if you have you'll regret ever having tangled with me," he said viciously.

"No of course I haven't, but listen, please." The last thing she wanted was to be reduced to pleading, as she feared it would bring out the cruel side of his nature, and she had seen too much of that in the past; she knew she had to shock him into attention.

"It's Jason, I've killed him. I stabbed him." The words rushed out of her. Lorenzo sprawled himself untidily into an easy chair. On a side table stood a bottle of Nardini grappa, almost empty, and a grappa glass. His hand was reaching for the glass when her words reached him. His head had slowly turned and then, as her meaning penetrated his alcoholic haze, he jerked upright.

"You've what?" All trace of his evening drinking had vanished.

"He told me he was going to tell O'Donnell about us. I was sure he meant it. I had to silence him and it had to be permanent. What else could I have done?"

"Tell me," he had said, his voice now very quiet, cold and expressionless. He motioned her to another chair. "Tell me everything."

Annie sat, composed herself, then in as few words as possible, but not omitting any major detail, she went over the events at the apartment on the Via del Moro. Lorenzo gave her his full attention.

"I'm sure they believed me, Macbride and this Steve Cromarty, when I said it was in self-defence," she ended.

Lorenzo swigged down the remaining grappa, then sat in silence for several minutes, deep in thought, while Annie waited anxiously for him to respond. Finally, he pushed himself to his feet.

"Okay, it's done, so there's no point fretting about it. He's no great loss. You get home but stay by the phone. I'll go and see O'Donnell and I'll be in touch."

Annie left at once, extremely glad that Lorenzo had taken the news as calmly as he had. She walked two hundred yards from the block of flats before she picked up a cruising taxi.

Within minutes of Annie leaving his apartment, Lorenzo drove out from the underground parking area and headed for O'Donnell's private villa, which nestled in a hollow on the southern slopes leading up to the San Miniato church. He was not expecting it to be an easy meeting; O'Donnell was not that sort of person. However, the information he'd brought was received without any outward show of alarm, almost as if O'Donnell had had previous knowledge of it, he later thought, and, with almost indecent haste, an alteration to the plans had been concocted and set in motion.

Back in his apartment, Lorenzo phoned Annie. There were no preambles. "Be ready to move in the morning," he told her. "Have all your things with you and I'll pick you up. Eight o'clock beside the taxi area on the Piazza della Independenza. I'll give you the details then."

He rang off without waiting for an answer, and Annie

packed her bag. The schedule must be tight if he was prepared to come out to seek her, even if the Independenza was still a good three quarters of a mile from her cramped two-room flat in a block off the Santa Reperata. But even with a tight schedule, she knew there was no way he would have come to her door – it was more than his self-image could allow.

She set her alarm for six thirty and for no obvious reason, suddenly thought of Steve Cromarty. She found herself wondering what might have been if things had been different. She had enjoyed being in his company in San Gimignano, even though it was part of the job, and his controlled anger about the camera switch had excited her more than she would have admitted to anyone. She fell asleep with the hope that he would still feature in the revised plan.

The next morning she entered Piazza della Independenza through its main gateway only moments before Lorenzo eased his grey Mercedes into the kerb at the front of the waiting line of taxis. He kept the engine running as she threw her bag into the back and quickly clambered into the front passenger seat. Anticipating her pulling the door closed, he smoothly moved the car out into the rush-hour traffic circling the green-treed oasis. They struck lucky with each of the sets of traffic lights and in less than ten minutes, by taking the route round the station to avoid the Irish pub area, Lorenzo was approaching the Via del Moro from the Via Palazzuolo.

He parked outside a coffee and sandwich bar; the owner came out to protest, but then beat a hurried retreat when he saw who it was.

"I'll put you in the picture now before we go and pick up Cromarty, our helper," Lorenzo said as he'd switched off the engine. Annie didn't reply. She simply turned and gave him her full attention, although she felt a wave of annoyance sweep through her, not only at the way Steve had been referred to as a helper but at the tone Lorenzo had used when he said it.

"O'Donnell reckons it'll be best all round if we get you out of the way, because of the Jason business," said Lorenzo. "He swallowed your self-defence story, so that's okay. You and Cromarty are to travel as a couple of tourists. I'm to fly you to Belvès this morning, then he intends the two of you to drive on further north when he's made the necessary arrangements."

He stopped there for a moment, waiting for her reaction.

"And how does this affect our plan? Will it be safe for us to go on with it?" she asked, concern etched on her face.

"There's no need to worry. I've had time to think it through and there's nothing in this that we can't go along with. We'll just divert later, that's all."

"Perhaps we should scrap the whole idea now and wait for another run."

"That wouldn't be a good idea. First, it's unlikely there'll ever be another run like this and, second, you seem to have forgotten that some people have already shelled out considerable sums and a fair bit has come our way already. They're not the sort who would take kindly if we renegued."

Annie made no reply, but her continued anxiety showed as she involuntarily twisted her mouth and nervously chewed her bottom lip.

"In any case," he continued lightly, "I'll be on hand. O'Donnell wants me to play a watching role for him." He smiled. "Little does he know what I'll really be watching for."

He started the car, pulled round into the Via del Moro and parked outside number 11. Before they got out, he put a reassuring hand on Annie's shoulder.

"Believe me, the plan will work. It can be done and we can do it," he said, then added, "with some assistance from Mr Cromarty."

Two minutes later they had entered the apartment and were informing Steve of his changed travelling arrangements. Lorenzo's confidence in their plan still holding up, despite the changed circumstances, could hardly have been more badly misplaced. But he was not to know that ten minutes before he'd arrived at O'Donnell's villa the previous night, O'Donnell had received a phone call from Macbride; then, ten minutes after he had left with the altered schedule, Macbride was being greeted in the sumptuous living room by an extremely affable Sean O'Donnell.

"I hope I haven't stopped you from having an early night," said O'Donnell.

Macbride simply shrugged. "I've had time to consider the news you gave me," continued O'Donnell, "and I rather think a little trip would do me good, don't you? Get away from all this for a while."

He vaguely wafted an arm around the room, as if to suggest that it had too many inadequacies to support any form of civilised living. Macbride moved across to a large drinks cabinet, pondered over the choice, then poured a generous measure of Sarpa di Poli grappa for each of them. He handed a glass to O'Donnell.

"Where've you got in mind?" he asked. The question went unanswered for the moment; O'Donnell was too intent on pursuing his own line of reasoning. Then he nodded at his glass and took a first careful, appreciative sip.

"I fancy this bringing in of Cromarty is going to flush something out of the woodwork," he eventually said. "And who knows, it may be starting already."

He quickly outlined the new arrangements he had

made with Lorenzo which Steve, Annie and Lorenzo would be following the next day. As O'Donnell talked, Macbride gave the impression of not being too concerned; he was being used as a sounding board, he wouldn't be directly involved.

He looked at the superb view from the large picture window; on the higher part of the slope was the silhouetted outline of the former monastery lit by discreet floodlights, and below that were well-tended gardens. Not quite the same as the rat's view of cold flagstones he usually looked out on. But O'Donnell's final sentence focused his attention and cut short any further odious comparisons regarding their respective living conditions.

"I've arranged for us both to be flown out ten minutes after them. I reckon at least one of them needs to be watched, and we'll be there to do the watching. It could be most interesting."

"The change will probably do me good," Macbride said, injecting some enthusiasm into his voice. Macbride had no safe way of informing Steve that he and O'Donnell would also be travelling to Belvès in the morning, nor of telling him that it might be their main purpose had changed. Sean O'Donnell's disclosure that he was looking to root out one of his own trusted team whom he now suspected of going over was not only news but bad news. It looked now as though the whole purpose of bringing in Steve wasn't to use a new route but that he was, in some way, to be used as a decoy. If that was the case, then all they could do was go along with it and come out clean, if they came out at all. On the bright side, it might give O'Donnell further proof of his usefulness to him. On the other hand, it might be that he was still intending to move the stuff; for Steve's sake he hoped he was, as it could possibly give him some sort of bargaining power if things went wrong. Macbride had a high regard for Steve's resourcefulness, but he knew it would have to be well laced with luck.

CHAPTER TEN

Despite his tiredness Steve slept fitfully, partly because his brain was in overdrive regarding the loyalties of Annie and Macbride, and partly because the storm continued to spiral around the city for the greater part of the night. The early rays of the dawn arrived without him being any nearer to knowing if he could trust one or both of them. At least there was the hint of an improvement in the weather, and by the time he was fully awake the sun was already warming the corrugated rose-pink, roof tiles and giving fair warning that it would be in control again today.

Before having a quick wash he glanced behind the settee to see how Jason was doing. "Quiet night, condition unchanged" could have been the bulletin given out on him if anyone had been interested enough to enquire, he thought.

He was just coming out of the bathroom when there was a knocking on the outside door; not loud, but insistent.

Probably Macbride's body-disposal squad, he thought, as he released the inside deadlock.

He was wrong. Annie entered the room, followed at close quarters by Lorenzo, and there was a distinct air of urgency about them both.

"I wasn't expecting you this early," he said, then, turning his full attention to Annie, he added, "but you're certainly welcome."

"There's no time for social chat, Steve," she said. "There's been a change made to the plans. We're leaving in half an hour. Flying to France."

"We? Who's we?"

"The three of us. Lorenzo's flying us out."

"So he does more than just mind coats for O'Donnell and take arty-crafty snapshots for you." Steve couldn't resist the jibe. It was fortunate that Annie was standing between the two of them.

"I think you two have to call off the war," she said. "You're meant to be on the same side." She moved past Steve, sliding her hand down his arm as she did so, and coolly sat down on the settee where less than eight hours earlier she had tearfully given her version of the event that led to Jason's death. It seemed the stabbing of a would-be rapist had left no deep psychological scars on her - no need for a session or two on a therapy couch. Steve mentally complimented her on her acting ability; or had he been the only one fooled? Or the only one who had to be fooled? Had Macbride been in on it from the start?

The doubt which had surfaced the previous night after he'd examined the hessian sack was not being blown away by this sudden change in plan; the fact that it was O'Donnell's plan that was being changed only complicated the matter further. However, he didn't feel he had much option other than to go along with it.

Strangely the presence of Lorenzo was reassuring and made it more acceptable; hadn't they said he was close to O'Donnell? He was also, at that precise moment, close to Steve.

"She talks a lot of sense for an Irish girl," he said, with just the faintest hint of a smile. Steve nodded; a truce, even if fragile and perhaps only temporary, had been born.

"Can you get your things together in the next quarter of an hour?" asked Annie.

"No problem with the stuff here," answered Steve, "but I've got a bag at the railway left luggage."

"Give me the ticket and I'll collect it for you," said Annie, half rising from the settee.

"No, I'm prepared to act out the innocent visitor," he countered. "I'll collect my own things, thanks."

Annie glanced at Lorenzo, then shrugged. "All right, but get back here as quick as you can."

"In ten minutes, no later," added Lorenzo from behind

the settee, where he had moved round to view Jason's corpse. From the over-emphasis on the last two words he was obviously intent on asserting his position.

"As you're flying us out, I don't suppose there's any danger of you leaving without me," put in Steve as he moved to the door.

Annie, anxious to avoid any flare-up between them, quickly answered for Lorenzo. From the look he shot across to her, she spoke out of turn. "Our air traffic man comes off duty just after nine. We're already logged through to Cagliari."

The name stopped Steve in his tracks. "Cagliari?" he repeated. "I'm not the world's best geographer, but I know that's not in France." He looked across at Lorenzo for an explanation. Lorenzo gave an exaggerated sigh, then delivered a partial explanation in a barely-veiled condescending tone.

"At nine five this morning four identical aircraft will take off from four different airports and, by avoiding certain beacons, they will be able to land at places other than their own, original logged destinations. That way we will not be followed. We will land at Belvès airfield in south-west France. One of the other planes will land at Cagliari. It's straightforward and simple."

"But what about radar checks on the beacons?" asked Steve. This time Lorenzo's face split wide, with a grin revealing a two-tooth gap on the left side.

"This is Italy, Mr Cromarty. I am an aviator, not an airline pilot. Aviators don't need to fly by beacons. This is accepted. Radar is only interested in the big boys or military. As long as we don't get in their way, we can fly pretty well where we want."

"You'd better hurry," put in Annie to Steve. "We must leave here by eight forty at the latest."

"Don't worry, I'll be back by then. I wouldn't want to miss the great aviator's show," said Steve. He left them and made his way through the courtyard and into the street. There was no sign of Macbride on the arcaded corner so there was no opportunity of sounding him out about the change in plan; he would just have to go along with it and see what emerged.

There were very few tourists around yet, so as he hurried up to the station, he only had to negotiate his way round solemn-faced office workers coming into the central area of the city to earn their daily crust. He wondered how many of them would give up the possibility of a secure pension in twenty or thirty years' time and be parcel couriers. It would probably depend on what was in the parcel, and that he didn't know for sure.

Without thinking, he tapped the camera which he'd managed to squeeze into his money belt and grimaced. He must relearn, and quickly, not to do things like that.

At the railway station he went first to the information

area, where he spent a moment or two using the computer aid for journeys, then, satisfied, he made a note on the back of an envelope. From there he made his way to the left luggage room by way of a post box which stood just beside the manned police kiosk. He dropped the letter into the box just as he was passing a group of students who were milling around one of their number who was having a heated debate with a policewoman. He felt sure no one had seen him do it.

The letter had been written the previous night when doubt had begun to raise its insidious head. Because of the time factor, the addition he had just made had had to be on the back of the envelope: 'Florence… Cagliari (NO) Florence… Belvès (YES) –by air'. He knew that both that and the contents of the letter would be acted upon if, and this was something of a worry, the Italian postal system was reasonably efficient.

An even greater cause for concern was whether the address he'd used still forwarded marked mail. Twenty years before, he'd known for sure that no matter where he was he would get back-up if he made contact. But how long these channels were kept open he didn't know. All he could do was hope that he wouldn't need them or, if he did, that the channel was still operational. There was no point in dwelling on it, he thought; there was no alternative and he'd done what he could. This was when you had to trust that your lucky star wasn't having a day off.

He picked up his in-flight bag and made his way back through the underpass to the corner of the Piazza della Unita Italiana. From there he hurried along the side of the church grounds, stopping only to buy another boxed orchid at the stall near Macbride's corner; Macbride still wasn't in residence.

It was exactly eight-forty when he arrived back at the apartment. Annie and Lorenzo were waiting for him in a grey Mercedes parked ten yards down the street, Lorenzo behind the wheel. Steve got in the back and, as the car pulled smoothly away, he leaned forward and presented the orchid to Annie.

"To my favourite travelling companion," he said and was pleased to see her warm smile and the sparkle in her eyes as she turned to take it from him.

At the same time, in the driver's interior mirror, he saw a scowl momentarily cross Lorenzo's features. 'Keep lucky,' he thought, 'two birds with one stone.'

The drive to the small airport, which lay to the south west of the city, should have been a twenty-minute journey, but even though the roads still had the last of the morning rush hour traffic, Lorenzo, with a smooth display of fast driving, knocked almost five minutes off that time. In contrast the airport was hardly a hive of activity; most of the international flights used Pisa and the scheduled internal flights took place outward early morning and inward early evening. In fact most of the administrative staff seemed to have disappeared to resume their breakfasts after the eight-thirty Fokker 324 departure to Turin was safely away and Lorenzo was able to drive to within twenty yards of the six seater Cessna.

As soon as he'd stopped the car he half-walked, half-ran to the squat control tower cum briefing room. "We'd better get on board," said Annie, and together they stowed their bags on the plane and then settled themselves in separate seats on either side of the narrow aisle and waited for Lorenzo to join them.

"How trustworthy is this guy?" asked Steve, keen to do some quizzing in Lorenzo's absence.

"He's become very important to O'Donnell, so he's one hundred per cent," answered Annie. "That's why he's here."

"To keep an eye on us."

"No, to keep an eye on you. I'm also one hundred per cent in his eyes, at least I think so."

"So why this sudden change of plan? Macbride didn't know of it last night."

"Macbride doesn't know everything, despite what he would like you to believe." She smiled rather wistfully. "Anyway, after the problem of last night O'Donnell thought it would be better for me to leave quickly and, as we're supposed to be a couple of tourists, then you had to come along as well."

"You make me feel so wanted," said Steve ruefully.

"I didn't say you weren't," answered Annie warmly, "and the orchid was much appreciated."

"Good. So when do we drop off this gooseberry so we can be the loving couple?" "We don't. And don't think because I'm going all the way with you that I'll go..."

The sentence remained unfinished, as at that moment Lorenzo hauled himself into the pilot's seat. Steve leaned across the aisle and whispered in Annie's ear just before the engine exploded into life.

"Do you honestly think I'm that sort of man?"

She didn't answer but, as far as he could tell, her look said, 'Yes' and she didn't seem too displeased with the idea.

The take-off was smooth and Steve was impressed with Lorenzo's skill but, as soon as the plane was eased out of the climb and they were on level flight, he couldn't resist leaning forward and reminding him, "Top of the climb. Don't forget your pressure and temperature checks."

Lorenzo's head whipped round. "You fly?"

"Not for a while," answered Steve and left it at that.

The flight might have been described by some as uneventful in that the weather was good, there was little turbulence, and there were no in-flight movies to ignore. But one thing that couldn't be ignored was the scenery, which, for much of the time, was rushing past either fifty feet below them or fifty feet to the sides as Lorenzo took the pretty way along the valleys wherever possible. This guy could fly, thought Steve grudgingly. He called over Lorenzo's shoulder, "Let's hope there's not another aviator coming in the opposite direction." He put heavy emphasis on the word 'aviator'. But he was disappointed in that there was no obvious reaction.

They had reached the coast about half an hour before and there, instead of turning south towards Corsica and then Sardinia, Lorenzo had continued westwards; Cagliari was definitely not to be on their itinerary. They skirted the southern edge of the Alps and beneath them was the limestone area of the *garrigue*. Bare, grey rock outcrops swept beneath them with scattered and scattering groups of sheep or goats and small, stone cabins tucked into sheltered clefts. After a while trees gradually began to appear, poor stunted specimens, widely spaced at first then larger and more grouped until, in another twenty minutes, they were flying over great stretches of forest with only small patches of cultivated farmland.

Steve had long since been forced to admit to himself, although grudgingly, that Lorenzo was no slouch as an aviator and he'd been able to relax and enjoy the flight. A glance across at Annie and he saw that she too had every confidence in Lorenzo's ability to keep the plane from plastering itself over the landscape – she'd relaxed so much that she was fast asleep. Even cramped up as she was, he noted that she couldn't hide her beddable potential; he hoped they would be able to find time for more than just business.

As nothing could be done in that area at the moment he turned his attention back to the ground they were covering. It was now obvious that they were roughly following the course of a large river and Lorenzo, aware of Steve's attention, half turned and called to him, "That's the river Ceon." He pointed ahead and to the right. "We stay with it until it meets the Dordogne. From there it's four and a half minutes to Belvès. Remember you're a tourist, so that's Castelnau down there on the left; I think it belonged to the English one time."

As the plane made a sweeping turn to the south west the chateau made an impressive sight with the morning sun adding a golden-brown glow to the stonework.

Steve gently shook Annie's shoulder. "Wake up, girl. Time to start taking in the sights." She was awake in an instant, smiled at him, and then pulled herself upright. "Is it much further?" she asked.

"A matter of minutes, he says." Steve nodded at Lorenzo's back. "But smile, because at the moment we're part of the attractions."

Lorenzo had brought the plane even lower and they could clearly make out the faces of a number of tourists walking round the battlements; some of them even started to wave. Then they were over dense woodland once more and Steve was beginning to wonder about the sort of airport they were making for when Lorenzo turned round to him again and pointed down to an open, grassed area with a small, white stone building and a larger dark, wooden barn at the furthest end.

Steve had landed on grass strips before, but he would have felt happier if the field had had a bit more length to it. That wasn't his problem, but he needn't have worried, as Lorenzo made a smooth landing with only a couple of almost negligible bounces before running the aircraft up towards the buildings. The jolting over the sun-hardened corrugated field was far worse than the landing, almost enough to loosen tooth fillings, and then they were stopped.

Lorenzo switched off and they all unstrapped and waited. The sudden silence and lack of movement after the exhilaration and noise of the flight seemed strangely unreal.

"Looks as though we've picked the wrong day in the week," suggested Steve.

"We're two minutes early," said Lorenzo tetchily as he checked his watch.

"So we could have had another circuit round the castle," countered Steve.

"They're coming now," said Annie, who had been looking out of her side window.

The large double door of the barn had been opened and from the dark, shadowed interior two cars appeared, a

Citroen 2CV and a Volvo estate. They slowly made their way across to the plane and parked alongside. As they watched Annie surprised Steve by saying, "Well, this is where we part company with Lorenzo."

"Don't worry, I'll not be far away," the Italian answered as he jumped down and pulled his flight bag after him.

"Was that comment meant for me rather than you?" Steve asked Annie with a quizzical expression on his face.

"You're becoming paranoid," she answered.

"No, just obsessed. Anyway which car is for us?"

"Which do you think?" laughed Annie. "I mean we are supposed to be British tourists."

She made her way to the Volvo. By the time Steve had both their bags stowed in the back of the car Annie was behind the wheel, so he slipped into the passenger seat. Lorenzo, in the meantime, was evidently not in any particular hurry to move on. He had lit a cigarette and was leaning on the wing of the plane chatting to the men who'd brought the cars from the barn.

CHAPTER ELEVEN

"They're not giving us much of a send-off," observed Steve drily as Annie put the car into gear.

"Don't worry about it. Lorenzo knows where we're going," she replied as she drove carefully past the white-washed building, which obviously served as the control tower, and along the pot-holed dirt track which led from the airfield to a narrow tarmac road.

Steve looked keenly into the woods on either side; he had a distinct gut feeling that something was wrong. Lorenzo not being with them was unexpected, but that wasn't it. And then it struck him. It was inside the car, not outside.

"It's a right hand drive," he said. He gave her a moment or two, thinking she hadn't responded because she was concentrating on avoiding the potholes, but as soon as they were on the made-up road he repeated himself.

"I said it's a right-hand drive car."

"So?" said Annie, not in the least bothered by this revelation. "It makes sense, doesn't it? We're meant to be British tourists remember, and it's supposed to be our car."

"Yeah, but as the change of plan was only hatched after the Jason business of last night it just seems a bit coincidental, don't you think?"

Annie gave him a quick look and he thought he saw a fleeting expression of concern before she turned her attention back to the road.

"Steve, this organisation is bigger than you realise. I've long since given up being surprised at what they can produce, and at short notice." She turned to him and smiled. "After all, they found you didn't they?"

"Okay, I'm convinced." Steve nodded. But behind his smile he wondered who had found him and for what purpose. It brought back the question that had plagued him most of last night – was old, paunchy Macbride to be trusted any more than the delectable Annie? And to add to that, there was the question of the second plane - or was he indeed becoming paranoid as Annie had suggested?

A few minutes after they had landed, while they were getting themselves organised with the car, Steve had become aware of another light aircraft circling the airfield but making no attempt to land. Now, as they drove in the direction of Belvès, the enclosing woods made it impossible to see if that plane was still in the air. He made a quick, calculated decision.

"Stop the car, Annie."

"Why?" she made to protest, but he cut her off.

"If we're supposed to be tourists then I'm going to be the one doing the driving, and don't give me any crap about male chauvinism."

The steeliness of his tone convinced Annie that he was not going to be fobbed off. She stopped the car and they quickly changed places. Steve drove the car fast for about half a mile and then saw what he had been hoping for – an old hunters' track that led into the wood on the left hand side. He slewed the car into it and was pleased to see that it turned slightly back on itself. Within thirty yards the Volvo was well hidden from the road. Certainly anyone travelling from the airfield towards Belvès would not see them.

"I just need to make myself comfortable," he said. "I'll only be a few minutes." He got out of the car and made his way back along the track and round the bend. As soon as he was sure he was out of sight of Annie and the car's wing mirrors, he pushed his way through the trees, avoiding scattered clumps of low-growing brambles, until he could get a good view of the road they'd just travelled along. He waited and, as one minute stretched into another, he began to wonder if his hunch was wrong.

He had almost decided to take the opportunity to relieve himself as promised when he heard the car approaching. It came into view; a large, dark green Peugeot travelling at not much less than the speed he'd been doing himself. As Steve pulled himself back behind a tree he saw the driver quite clearly. It was a young male. Was it Lorenzo? He couldn't be sure. In the back of the car he could just make out two bulky men, and then it was past his hiding place.

Then, as luck would have it, as it went into the next bend one of the men turned as if to speak to the other and for a split second Steve saw in profile the unmistakeable face of Macbride. Steve was fairly sure the other passenger was O'Donnell.

He reckoned he had another sixty seconds at most before Annie would begin to doubt his reason for leaving the car. Running through even fairly open woodland while trying to avoid being seen is not the simplest of tasks, particularly under pressure of time, and he also had to make a wide detour to get round to the front of the vehicle. As he'd expected, when he reached the car Annie was looking over her shoulder back down the track and was unaware of his return.

Believing the opportunity might not come again, he made an on-the-spot decision. He took a couple of large gulps of air to steady himself, then wrenched the passenger door open and put his hands round her neck, almost jamming her head between the two front seats, before she had a chance to struggle. He leaned across her with his face close to hers.

"Annie, you're going to talk or you're going to die right here. Do you hear me?"

His voice was low but she heard it, and, as he pulled her up into a near-normal sitting position, his hands still squeezing her neck, she managed to give a slight nod. Her eyes were wide open - fear, or the pressure on her neck, or both - but she still had a measure of control that Steve couldn't help but admire.

He slowly released his hold with his right hand and with it grabbed her left forearm.

"Sit on your hand Annie and then the other one, and don't try anything you might regret." She quietly did as she was told, and he took his left hand from her neck.

"I'm going to be straight with you, girl" he said, still leaning into the car. "I have a good idea how Jason died and it wasn't how you said it was. This time I want you to be straight with me. Understand?"

She nodded again, but this time her eyes were on his face, searching for eye contact.

"I want answers to three questions," continued Steve, "so listen very carefully. One, who are you working for? Two, what's next on the agenda? Three, and this is the most crucial one for you, why should I believe you? And don't take all day over it."

"Okay," she said, swallowing with some difficulty and then licking her lips. "One, I don't know who I'm working for, but I'm working with Macbride. Two, we go into Belvès, then take the route north to Wimereux on the Channel, but I expect more details to be passed to us tonight or tomorrow by Lorenzo."

She stopped at that point and stared straight ahead through the windscreen. "And the third thing, the most important," he reminded her. "Why should I believe you?"

She turned a defiant face towards him and, almost unbidden, the words came rushing out. "Yes, I knifed Jason last night because if I hadn't he'd have brought everything down on Macbride's head by telling O'Donnell what he'd found out."

Perhaps Steve's expression still gave her cause for concern, as she quickly continued, "Believe me, I'm not an indiscriminate killer."

Steve wanted to believe her, as at that moment she was one of the most beautiful women he'd ever set eyes on; certainly the most beautiful killer, indiscriminate or not. He looked closely into her eyes.

"I want to believe you Annie, more than you could know," he said. Then, deciding he hadn't any other worthwhile option open to him, he added briskly, in a tone that belied his underlying doubts, "So now we're working together you'd better drive, as you know where we're going." He pushed her across into the driver's seat, helping her thighs over the gear lever.

"Ever the gallant," she said, with a wan smile.

"That's definitely me," he agreed.

She started the engine and slowly reversed the car along the track and out onto the road. He made no further comment for the next couple of miles, deliberately giving her time to fully recover her composure. He was interested to see how she would react to his revelation.

"By the way," he said casually, "O'Donnell and Macbride have already gone down into the town. When I was out of the car I saw them pass our hiding place back there."

There was an awful silence in the car. She didn't look at him, didn't speak, simply concentrated fixedly on the road ahead. But the colour had drained from her face. One deeply troubled girl, thought Steve.

★ ★ ★

O'Donnell and Macbride had been driven into the town, completely unaware of having been seen by Steve, and parked in the market square. At O'Donnell's direction the driver had carried their cases down to the Impasse de Cours. There they'd entered a flat with the name R. Larequaie written on a card beneath the bell push.

"Not the best of billets, but I've seen worse," Macbride said.

"It'll do us," O'Donnell answered. "In any case I don't think we'll be here too long."

★ ★ ★

Steve and Annie were now approaching the town. Steve had only the vaguest knowledge of the area and none at all about Belvès, but it was obvious to him, from the way she confidently threaded the car down into the outskirts of the upper part of the town, that Annie was no first-time visitor to the place.

As they approached the church, she turned along a narrow side street before dropping down a gentle slope which brought them to a car park at the side of the flag-bedecked Mairie building. As she switched off the engine an elderly couple came out of the building and Annie busied herself searching under the dashboard.

"There's no need to hide. They're not interested in us," said Steve as he watched them slowly making their way around the further corner while carefully scrutinising some sort of document which they'd obviously been given.

Annie ignored the comment. "We'll walk from here," she said, "so let's pick up the bags."

The walk took no more than two minutes and Steve noted with approval that the hotel she led them to was just the place that tourists working on a reasonable budget would look for.

"I'm pleased to see we're not slumming it with the riff-raff," he whispered to her as they stood waiting at the reception desk. "And, just as a matter of interest, not that it's any concern of mine of course, but where is Lorenzo going to be putting his head down tonight?"

Annie threw him a look, but at the same instant the desk girl suddenly arrived to check them in and her attention was diverted.

"We have a double room booked in the name of Martin," said Annie in comfortable French. She completed the necessary formalities. Steve's French was a touch rusty, but it didn't prevent him from getting the gist of what she'd said and he was well pleased with the prospect. Annie signed the hotel register as the girl selected a key from a drawer under the counter and pushed it across to them.

"Room G. First floor, on the front," she said.

As Steve picked up the key and then their two bags, he was conscious of the girl's eyes on him. He'd already got her summed up as having potential, a good first reserve, but any further thoughts on those lines were stillborn as Annie asserted her role.

"Be careful you don't strain anything, darling," she said. "That might spoil things." She still spoke in French, so Steve knew that the comment wasn't really meant for his ears. Once more he had to admire the ease with which she coped with the situation. He was sure that Macbride and

O'Donnell hadn't been on her schedule for this trip, and yet already she had thrown off any signs of anxiety.

As they climbed the stairs to the first floor, he wondered how Lorenzo would have reacted to the news. Unless of course he had known about this before them; they had left him at the airfield, so he must have seen the second plane land. He might have seen its passengers; he might even have been the driver of the car that took them in the direction of Belvès.

However, speculation on all of those possibilities ended when they reached Room G. It was just as he'd hoped it would be – a huge double bed which took up almost half the floor space, a large wardrobe and two simple hard-backed chairs. To his mind no caring colleen would condemn a man to sleep on those; the bed would have to be for both of them. But any discussion on that had to wait.

"I'm having the first shower," Annie announced, without any preamble, as she started to pull her sweater over her head. Steve sat on the edge of the bed, lit a cigarette, and watched the floor show as she deftly stripped down to her underwear, showing not the slightest hint of embarrassment.

"Clothes don't become you, do you know that?" he said. She made no reply, but lightly skipped across to him, took a quick drag on the cigarette, kissed him full on the lips, and then made her way into the bathroom.

Steve allowed himself to indulge in some pleasantly erotic daydreaming for a few minutes, and then walked across to the heavily netted window. As he pulled the net to one side and opened the window a church clock began to strike eleven o'clock. Probably time to do a bit of wandering around, he thought, if for nothing else other than to show that he was still his own man rather than a strung puppet.

He tried the bathroom door and it opened to his touch; Annie must be a trusting soul, or perhaps she didn't really see him as a red meat guy – even more of a reason for taking his own line of action. He was surprised to see that she was already towelling herself down.

"I'm off to do some sightseeing," he announced.

"Don't you think it would be better if we went together?" She seemed genuinely concerned. "People might think it odd. And you don't know the place."

"Don't worry. I'm a big boy now. I'll be back within an hour." He closed the bathroom door before she could make any further protest. Before he left the bedroom he carefully positioned his bag on the faded, patterned carpet, well away from where Annie might have any need to move it. In this game trust was the main road to oblivion, he reminded himself as he made his way downstairs.

Half-hoping the desk girl might be around, he loitered in the entrance hallway, idly picking up a selection of the tourist literature from the table.

"Can I be of assistance, sir?" The question came in a startlingly deep voice from behind the corner pillar of the bar. Steve slowly turned to face the questioner. He was a well-built, smartly-dressed black man, about thirty years of age, who looked as though he wouldn't be out of place among the Santa Novella Square crowd back in Florence. The smile he gave was cold and business-like, almost menacing if Steve had been of either a nervous or over-imaginative disposition.

"Not really," he said. "I was hoping to make the acquaintance of the desk girl." A sprinkling of truth would not do his image any great harm.

"I'm afraid you're just too late. Rita takes an early lunch on weekdays."

"So she works late evenings to make up?" ventured Steve.

"Yes, but she's always busy." This was accompanied by a smile which was as good as saying "too busy for you". Steve was not impressed with the guy's attitude; with his teeth, yes, but not his attitude. Since when did the welfare of staff come before the consideration of paying guests, he wondered.

"If you want for anything, anything at all," the man continued, "just ask for me."

"And you are?" Steve was pleased to be able to make it clear with those three simple words that he considered the man in front of him to be an utter nonentity.

"The manager, Signor Barloni," he replied, stiff with wounded self-esteem.

"Thank you, I'll bear you in mind," Steve replied, with a smile as false as Signor Barloni's had been. "Now I'll see what your town's made of." He ended the conversation by pushing out into the heat and the glare.

★ ★ ★

The security team that had been given the task of following Steve were a well-trained, professional outfit and over the next thirty-six hours his movements were well covered. They did lose track of him once, after he and Macbride had crossed the Ponte alla Carrala, but they picked him up again on his return to the Via del Moro. All in all they were reasonably happy with their work, although they had crucially missed seeing him placing the camera in the window box and were only aware of it when they saw him retrieve it late that evening after Macbride and the girl had left the apartment. The two who had missed this opportunity decided it would be in their best interests not to mention this in their report.

The team had much more tangible success when they followed Steve to the railway station, where he picked up his bag and, despite a milling throng of noisy, aggrieved students, they saw him post his letter. By the time Steve had rejoined Annie and Lorenzo for the drive to the airport, the letter was in the hands of Superintendent Asconi and fifteen minutes later he was talking to his counterpart in Périgeux. As a result of all this activity the arrival of Steve and Annie in Belvès was known to more than Lorenzo, Macbride and O'Donnell. All the hotels in the town which had pre-booked arrivals for that day, and there were only three of them, were covered and personnel were in place within the hour. For them it was simply a matter of waiting to see where they would show up and then tightening the arrangements at that point.

The call from Rita marking the arrival of Annie and Steve at the hotel was, therefore, not unexpected. But what their preparations did not cover was the appearance on the scene of O'Donnell and Macbride. They constituted two loose cannons which might somehow wreck all their plans – plans which at that precise moment were working so remarkably smoothly that Stefan Barloni had already, albeit temporarily, taken the place of Roger Larequaie as hotel manager before Steve had finished arranging the position of his case in the bedroom. However, because of the short notice involved, corners had had to be cut and vital information had not been made available to them; consequently their plan was seriously flawed. As well as having been unaware of the arrival of Macbride and O'Donnell, even more crucially, they had not been informed by central records of Larequaie's previous contacts with Sean O'Donnell. Roger Larequaie, who considered himself to be his own man, had a distinctly jaundiced view of most forms of state intervention and he was not a staunch supporter of the local gendarmerie. He had also reached the age where he was more than happy to have his pension fund topped up with regular, hefty payments in return for providing safe accommodation without troubling to ask any awkward questions.

As a result, when he was brusquely informed by an arrogant, non-local, half-Italian from regional security that he had to vacate his own hotel, he had no compunction about making his way to the small flat which O'Donnell had provided for him in the Impasse de Cours. His intention was to get a message off to O'Donnell in Florence, but when he arrived at the flat he found there was no need for phone calls; O'Donnell was there in person, together with another man whom he vaguely remembered meeting several years ago. The information he brought of third party intervention wasn't good news for Sean O'Donnell, but he was not one to be easily panicked; on careful consideration, he was of the opinion that the advantage still lay with him – he was the only one who knew the real reason why this run was taking place.

He moved into the inner room and, out of earshot of both Macbride and Larequaie, he telephoned Lorenzo. The owner of Au Bon Temps answered in the sibilant, but sensual, tones which had so attracted Lorenzo on his first visit there three years before.

"Hello, Au Bon Temps Antiquités ?"

"Get Lorenzo on the line," snarled O'Donnell. "I know he's there."

"Yes, my friend Lorenzo is here. But he is very tired, he is resting."

O'Donnell was neither interested in nor sympathetic to Lorenzo's tiredness, and he made that abundantly clear. "Tell him he'll be resting more peacefully than he would like if he doesn't get on the end of this phone now. Don't talk, just get him."

It had the desired effect. Lorenzo listened intently. He was no fool. On the face of it he had accepted O'Donnell's sudden decision to come to Belvès himself, "to see things through," as he had put it. He now readily agreed with the necessity of making the acquaintance of this 'manager' Barloni.

A call from one Italian to another and their first brief meeting was arranged. Their next meeting, the same evening, was to have terminal consequences for Stefan Barloni, who had also found the owner of the antique shop to be to his particular liking, and Lorenzo had never been one to share. After the phone call O'Donnell told Larequaie to have a drink in a nearby bar but be back in half an hour as he would have a job for him.

After he had left O'Donnell began pacing around the small living room, pressing his right fist into his beard. It was obvious to Macbride that O'Donnell was really in a quandary, struggling to make sense of the new information he'd been given. But he also knew that it was not his place to comment, and the next move should not be instigated by him; Sean O'Donnell was the man in charge, the man who pulled the strings. The last thing Macbride wanted was to give any impression of being anxious about the outcome.

O'Donnell started talking, almost as if to himself. "We could pull out now, all of us, or just you and me," he said. He stopped and looked at Macbride, but he was not seeking an opinion. "If we do that, what have we learned? Nothing." He continued pacing. "Remember the main purpose of the exercise, Macbride?"

Macbride nodded. But it wasn't his problem; his whole attitude indicated weariness and disinterest. "To test the loyalty of two operatives," he answered.

"Exactly," said O'Donnell. "And it may be that this slight complicating factor might test it even more. I need to know. I must know. If they have already sold out, or if they haven't but can't handle this extra pressure, they are useless to us."

"Is Cromarty still going to be of any use?" asked Macbride. O'Donnell continued his pacing.

"I think Cromarty is good, maybe very good. But it is possible he might have to be sacrificed."

Macbride shrugged. "It's a part he's played before."

O'Donnell again stopped in his tracks and looked at Macbride; for just the briefest instant he thought of this man sacrificing his wife and now being prepared to sacrifice Cromarty. He wondered who else he would be ready to turn his back on. And then he made the decision.

"We'll give it another twenty-four hours."

"Give them enough rope, eh?" suggested Macbride.

"That's it, enough rope," said a smiling O'Donnell. "Someone just might hang themselves. But I have a feeling Lorenzo might be trying to be one step ahead. I need to check the contents of the camera."

CHAPTER TWELVE

For the second time in three days Steve was standing in a foreign town trying to decide which route to take. But this time he was also cursing himself for being so tetchy with Signor Barloni. It was hardly the reaction of someone who was supposed to be on a tourist trip with his girlfriend; he'd better get into the part and stay in it. In any case, what sort of a state must he be in if he was reduced to scoring points off hotel managers?

Across the road, almost directly opposite the hotel front, was the entrance to a narrow street lined by tall buildings whose ground floors were taken up by shops. As well as looking as though it was one of the main streets in the town, it also looked invitingly cool, so he made his way over. Just as he was about to step into its welcome shade he glanced across to the car park where they'd left the car less than half an hour ago – there were several cars there now, all of them French registered, which was to be expected. But what did give him food for thought was that there was no Volvo. Well, there was no point in worrying about a missing car, especially as it wasn't his.

With that not altogether consoling thought, Steve set off up the Rue Jacques Manchotte, determined to play the tourist for an hour. There were few people around; some solitary, elderly women, baskets over their arms, doing the day's shopping, and three old men sitting on wicker chairs outside the Maison de la Presse, immersed in their papers. None of them gave him even a glance.

Ten minutes of strolling and window gazing brought him to the Place d'Armes with its fine, medieval, open-sided market hall. At one corner of the square was a branch of the Crédit Agricole, and he took the opportunity to use his plastic at the hole in the wall to fill his wallet – a present for Annie might work to his advantage, he thought, or perhaps the overworked Rita might appreciate the attentions of a well-heeled Brit. Old buildings had never given him much of a kick, no matter what their provenance – as far as he was concerned he wasn't going to waste part of his life looking at what others had managed to do with their chance. And in any case he still had more than a surfeit from San Gimignano to work out of his system.

However, he had a part to play, so he forced himself to wander slowly along the Rue des Ramparts and the Rue du Roi Charles V. There he stopped and, feigning genuine interest, examined the elegantly-carved doorway of the ancient hospital. It struck him then that a bona fide tourist wouldn't have ventured out without their camera, and he wondered if at that very moment a frantic search was being made to try and locate the one he'd left in the hotel. He felt reasonably confident that it was safe.

He made his way back to the main square, where he ordered a beer at a parasolled table at the only café that seemed to be functioning, and quietly observed the activity around him. The church clock struck the half-hour; a distant dog barked excitedly; two pigeons made a clattering flight through the market hall; and a plump Frenchman in baggy cords, navy sweater and beret, and glasses, giving a good impression of a prematurely-aged owl, crossed the square and disappeared down the Rue Foucastel on the corner of which stood Au Bon Temps – Antiquités.

And some people could put up with this and not be blown out of their minds, thought Steve.

Then in that same instant, with his eyes still focused on the antique shop corner, he saw Lorenzo in the shop doorway, talking animatedly with someone inside the shop.

Steve pulled out one of the tourist brochures he'd picked up in the hotel foyer and busied himself with it in such a way as to give him some sort of shield in case Lorenzo should look his way. It was unnecessary; Lorenzo was too involved in his conversation, and even at a distance Steve could see he was agitated and having to make an effort to keep control. Then suddenly he came out of the shop and made his way round the same corner as the old Frenchman had done.

The person Lorenzo had been talking to moved into Steve's line of vision; he was black and could have passed for the twin brother of Signor Barloni, even on a clear day. That bothered Steve more than he would have expected. After all, if Barloni did have a link with Florence, then why shouldn't he know Lorenzo? Half an hour ago he'd given Steve the distinct impression that he was on duty at the hotel, so why would he leave his post to meet up with him elsewhere in the town? Were the tentacles of O'Donnell's organisation at work even in this quiet backwater?

For a moment Steve considered rushing back to the hotel to see who was looking after the place in Barloni's absence. Instead he decided to follow Lorenzo once he'd seen Barloni disappear back into the shop; he reckoned it might be useful to know what Lorenzo was doing when he wasn't keeping Annie in his sights.

He quickly covered the ground to the corner, but Lorenzo was already out of sight. However, as the old Frenchman was also nowhere to be seen, he felt sure that somewhere, not too far down the street, there must be a side opening leading off it. Hurrying on, he found he was right. There was a narrow lane running down the back of the same shops which he'd walked along earlier, and Lorenzo was about fifty yards along it and not dawdling. Even if Lorenzo did not lead him anywhere interesting, Steve knew he would be heading back in the general direction of the hotel.

He had just convinced himself that he'd made the right decision when suddenly Lorenzo took a right turn. Steve decided to take the risk and follow. If Lorenzo was waiting for him around that corner, he'd fob him off with some sort of story; he'd always been good at that.

When he reached the place where Lorenzo had turned in, he found it was no more than a gap between the two buildings, barely more than two feet wide, which sloped up to the main street, the Rue Jacques Manchotte, and then continued but widened on the far side, where it seemed to end in a high, blank stone wall. Lorenzo was already in the cul de sac and was stepping into a doorway on the left-hand side.

There didn't seem to be much point in hurrying now, so Steve just strolled up to the main street. There were more people around than half an hour before, so he idly gazed around, giving the best impression he could of a tourist, gawping up in admiration at the old carved stone window surrounds on the two floors above street and shop level.

Bringing his attention back to the part that really interested him, he saw that the shop on the corner of the Impasse de Cours was empty. Its window shelf was littered with an assortment of artefacts ranging from arrowheads to crossbow bolts, and behind this collection was a large cardboard display giving a pictorial view of what the town was thought to have been like six hundred years ago.

Not much different from now, he thought, as he peered into the window trying to see round the display board. All he could see was a small area which was totally empty, and two internal doors which were closed.

He slowly drifted around into the cul de sac and made his way down to the door where he'd last seen Lorenzo. There was a small electric bell push, but he didn't think he'd gain anything other than trouble if he used it. Beneath it, in a plastic holder, was a hand-written name card – 'R. Larequaie'.

Before he retraced his steps to the main street he checked out the end wall of the cul de sac and mentally agreed with its Impasse name. It was certainly not the place to run into if you were being chased by heavies. He then started back for the hotel, as he knew Annie would be expecting him shortly and there didn't seem to be anything further to be gained hanging around here.

When he reached the end of the street, he noticed that the Volvo was back in the place where they'd left it. It was obviously now a sitting duck or a tail tag, and he wondered which.

However, thoughts on that were pushed to one side when across the road, he saw several people standing outside the main entrance of the hotel. Annie was amongst them and, as he reached the group, she made her way over to him.

"What's the problem?" he asked.

"There was a fire alarm ten minutes ago," she explained, taking his arm. "We had to evacuate the building."

"It's just as well you weren't still in the shower," he replied with a smile.

"Just another example of my natural sense of timing."

As they were speaking, it was becoming obvious that the general mood of the group was beginning to change from mild excitement to one of slight annoyance at having to wait in the main street while apparently nothing was being done in the hotel.

"They're a bit short on the smoke, never mind the flames," remarked Steve, with only a gentle trace of sarcasm. There was no opportunity for Annie to reply, as even as Steve was speaking Rita appeared. Right on cue, thought Steve.

"I'm sorry for keeping you out here so long," she said. "The problem has now been sorted out." She motioned for them all to re-enter the hotel. As soon as they were back in their room Steve surreptitiously checked the position of his case – as he'd expected, it had been moved. But by whom? Because of the fire alarm evacuation it could have been by someone other than Annie. He decided to leave mentioning it until later. No point in perhaps ruining a beautiful friendship before it had really been given the chance to get off the ground. If it had to be given that chance, then now seemed as good a time as any.

"I don't suppose I could persuade you that we really should go to bed now after our long journey," he suggested.

"For once you're right. Supposing that, I mean," she added hurriedly. But Steve was sure her tone had a touch of regret in it.

"Well do you have any better ideas?" he asked, "or do we just sit around and wait for Lorenzo, the messenger, to deliver?"

"No, I wish it was just that," she said.

"So what is it then?"

"When I was standing outside the hotel, about five minutes after we'd been ushered out, Macbride suddenly appeared. Large as life, never said how or why he was here. He just walked up to me as if we were back in Florence and said that we had to be ready to move tomorrow morning, early."

"Wasn't that what you'd expected?"

"For us and probably Lorenzo, yes. But Macbride said he'd be coming along as well."

"Don't worry about it," said Steve. "I reckon they've heard about my reputation when escorting young females. It'll have made them realise that Lorenzo will need some help keeping an eye on us."

"I don't know what to think," she answered. For the first time Steve thought she looked young, alone and vulnerable; whatever she was involved in, it was coming off the rails.

"But you've been told to get me out for the day. Am I right?"

It was a shot in the dark, but Annie's wide-eyed look confirmed it even before she nodded.

"Yes. Macbride said O'Donnell wanted you out of Belvès for a few hours and they left me to arrange it. But how did you know that?"

"Because I assume they didn't find what they were looking for," he answered.

"When?"

"Come on Annie, what do you take me for? It was a bogus fire alarm that was set off to get you out of the room. They knew I wasn't here as Signor Barloni had already seen me off on my tourist jaunt and…"

"Who is this Signor Barloni?" broke in Annie.

"You mean you haven't been introduced to the manager yet? The keeper of Rita, the desk girl, and all her charms?"

"I've stayed here several times and I'm sure it's French owned and French managed. It's been in the family for several generations," answered Annie with a puzzled look on her face.

"The manager you knew wasn't called Larequaie by any chance, was he?" It was another wild shot and he had no idea if it would hit a target and even if it did where it might lead.

"Yes, how did you know?"

"Well it wasn't any clever detective work, I'm sorry to say. I just happened to see the name on some hotel notepaper in the lobby downstairs."

He was pleased and relieved to see that she accepted the lie; he thought it best not to tell her how he had followed Lorenzo to the Larequaie doorway in the cul de sac. The more information he had which wasn't shared the better he'd feel.

"What would this Barloni person have been looking for?" she asked, pulling the conversation back to what interested her.

"Surely you haven't forgotten the camera," he replied. "The one Lorenzo switched at San Gimignano, with a little help from you as I remember. It's all about that".

"But it doesn't make sense."

"Unless Barloni is not playing for the same side", suggested Steve, but he didn't elaborate on that. Then in a brighter tone he said, "It would be nice to have answers, Annie, but it looks as though we'll just have to be patient. In the meantime let's just do what you were told to do – take me out for the day, then back for bed. We'll try to make some sense of it all later."

"I'm not promising to go along with all of that," she smiled.

"Do you mean you still might prefer Macbride, or perhaps a reincarnated Jason, to me?"

It had been intended as a light throwaway remark, but he had misjudged the fragile basis of their relationship. There had been times in his past when he had been accused of rushing things and assuming too much. This came back to him rather forcefully as, for the second time in forty eight hours, she flung a punch at him. But this time Steve was quicker and he moved inside the blow and grabbed her to him in a bear hug.

Annie gasped and, as he slowly released his hold, she looked up at him. Steve took her face in both hands and kissed her.

"Annie, I think you're just what I need," he whispered to her. At the same time he wondered if they were both being used, and by whom.

★ ★ ★

Due to the presence of Barloni and Rita in the hotel during the fire alarm O'Donnell was unable to find the camera, so it was necessary to make another arrangement. Macbride was dispatched to inform Annie that she had to take Steve out for the day, and he was touched by a faint pang of jealousy when she was obviously not displeased at the prospect. Larequaie, without an hotel to run and therefore with time on his hands, was given the task of following them, more to get him out of Belvès than with any real need for information about their jaunt. Had Steve known this, the over-zealousness of Larequaie would have given him great cause for concern. But excitement had come late into the Frenchman's life and, given this opportunity, he wasn't going to pass up on it.

CHAPTER THIRTEEN

Barely twenty minutes later, with what Steve thought was unseemly haste, they left the hotel; Annie was either very frightened, or simply anxious to do O'Donnell's bidding. Steve took the philosophical view and saw it as an opportunity to get to know her better. As she had already said, there might not be many other chances.

There was no sign of either Barloni or Rita in the hotel lobby. They were trusting souls, he thought.

Annie was obviously on the same wavelength. "If we'd known we could have had enough shampoo sachets to last us the whole trip," she said with a quick laugh.

He took her hand as they walked across to the car park. When they reached the car Annie made no comment about the Volvo's position, although Steve was fairly certain it hadn't been returned exactly to where they had left it. She took the wheel and they headed out of town, but in the opposite direction from the one they'd taken from the airfield.

"How do you know this area so well?" asked Steve, settling himself in the passenger seat in a manner which suggested that he for one was going to enjoy the excursion. As the reply took some time in coming, he glanced across at her. He knew why he was not only prepared to spend several hours doing the tourist things but positively looking forward to them. His lucky star was evidently still prepared to make the occasional appearance.

At last she answered. "The first time I came here was almost four years ago. With Macbride and Leila."

"Leila. Would that be the same…?" There was no need for him to finish the question as Annie nodded and broke in. "Yes. Leila was killed in the explosion at the Irish Pub the day you arrived."

"Two days ago," he said vaguely.

"It seems longer than that," she said quietly. "A lifetime ago." Her face was tense. She momentarily screwed shut her eyes as if to block out the memory.

Steve gave her time to compose herself before asking more. He tried to put a soft edge to his voice, but even to his own ears it sounded brutal and callous; he was forcing her to relive deeply painful memories, reopening wounds that were hardly yet beginning to heal.

"So four years ago Leila wasn't considered to be expendable. Is that right?"

She took several deep breaths, threw back her head and

then turned to glare at him, but in reality she wasn't looking at him; her gaze was focused far back into the past.

The car was picking up speed and Steve cast a quick, anxious glance at the road. The movement brought her back from her reverie to concentrate on her driving again.

"Expendable?" she said in a thin, wistful voice. "No, not then."

Another silence, but this time she was gathering herself. When she continued, her voice was stronger and the sadness had been replaced by a mixture of sarcasm and cynicism.

"Leila was Macbride's wife."

"Wife! Macbride!" exclaimed Steve incredulously. "Never."

He was completely taken aback by this. The Macbride he had known had never been one to enter into permanent relationships. Tied knots and signed registers were not for him, and from what he had seen since meeting up with him again it was the same Macbride. But even as he thought this, he couldn't see any reason for Annie to be spinning him a yarn.

"Yes, she was his wife," Annie repeated. "A few weeks before we came here they were married in a civil ceremony. The only thing that wasn't right about the arrangement was me — to fit me in I was supposed to be their daughter."

"The bastards," Steve muttered to himself. For a while, he stared out of the side window, but without really noticing the countryside they were passing through. He was thinking only of Macbride, the beer-swilling, foul-mouthed bastard who had left him to rot in an African prison for eight years, then arranged for him to be the fall guy in an explosion that killed innocent civilians, among them his own wife, who had somehow become expendable. There were easier ways of ending a relationship, he mused.

So what could the motive be behind Macbride's actions? Not any sort of idealism, as he avoided that like the plague. It had to be money, and now Steve was involved in it and was once more working with him. It wasn't the scenario he would have wished for, but what horrified him most of all was that, in place of the feeling of disgust and revulsion, a thin frisson of pleasure had crept unbidden into his brain.

It was Annie who brought him out of his reverie by continuing with her story of four years ago.

"We'd been sent here, I presume by O'Donnell, although that was never said to me, to check out a storage place for an arms shipment," she said. "I think there'd been some problems and they needed to hole things up in France for a while until it could be moved down to Bordeaux and then onto a trawler."

"And where was this place?" he asked, only mildly interested, as after all it was four years ago and he didn't see how it could fit into their present situation. "You could hide a regiment in this lot," he continued, waving a hand at the vast areas of woodland that the road was winding through.

"It was in the woods, but not the woods," she replied enigmatically.

"Annie, I gave up riddles when I came out of short pants."

She smiled. "You know I've often wondered what happened to boys at that age."

"Are you going to tell me or not?" he replied sharply.

"Better than that. I'm going to show you."

"Great, we've got a whole afternoon to kill. But I would appreciate having lunch first."

"The brute needs to be fed," she said with a light laugh he was pleased to hear. "Lunch in Monpazier should do us fine," she added after a glance at the dashboard clock.

"You're the one driving," said Steve, perfectly happy to let her organise the day.

The D53 would never be the busiest of roads, but at that time of day it was almost empty of traffic. Not really surprising, he thought, as, apart from the occasional hamlet and isolated farmhouse, there were few signs of people, and in any case, they were now well into lunchtime-siesta time.

The road twisted its way through woods of scrub oak, birch and chestnut, with just the odd straight stretch where Annie could put her foot down. At each of these sections Steve levered himself slightly forward to get into a position where he could use the wing mirror.

They were approaching the scattered houses making up the hamlet of Fongalop when he first saw the dark green Peugeot about two hundred yards behind them.

"I know you're anxious about getting to wherever you said for our lunch, but could you ease up a bit so I can appreciate the scenery?" he asked.

"I suppose we've got a bit of time to spare," she replied as she dropped the speed.

Two miles further on the land had flattened and the woodland edge was a greater distance from the road, which now ran through fields of sunflowers and maize with the odd pasture areas grazed by small herds of cattle. Steve sat up, giving a good impression of being interested in the area they were passing through, but it was what had appeared in the wing mirror which took up most of his attention.

The final run into Monpazier included another straight stretch, and there was the dark green Peugeot. Despite Annie having reduced their speed, Steve reckoned the Peugeot had maintained the same distance behind them. It was beginning to look very much as though some sort of tagging device had been placed on the Volvo during the time it had been moved from the Belvès car park.

"I think even you will be impressed with this place," said Annie. "I hope so, as it's one of my favourites. It was built by the English in the twelve hundreds and it's probably the best preserved of all the bastides in the area."

"Language, girl!" said Steve in mock disgust, dragging his attention away from the mirror. Annie smiled as she carefully negotiated the car through the narrow, arched gateway and down to the car park alongside the church. As they left the vehicle Steve shot a quick glance back up the street, but there was no sign of a dark green Peugeot. Perhaps he was becoming just a shade paranoid, he thought. After all, there was another world where people were going about their legitimate business with no interest in him or Annie.

"It's just on two," she said, and smiled as the church clock rang out to confirm it, "so we should be okay for food."

She led the way to where low-arched walkways provided shade and coolness to the shop fronts. The shops were all closed, being well into their three-hour siesta, so there was nothing to detain them. She pointed across to the far corner of the square.

"We'll go across there, where the tables have more shade," she said. As they left the cool protection of the arcades and stepped into the square, the heat met them like a furnace wall and the intense glare from the white stone gravel seared itself onto the eyeballs. Walking across the square Steve, with slitted eyes, forced himself to look around, and his philistine shell was immediately pierced. The buildings on all four sides looked as if they hadn't changed one iota from when they had first been constructed five or six hundred years before.

"The leader of a peasants' revolt was broken on the wheel here four hundred years ago," she said, as if feeling the need to make some sort of comment.

"Could have been yesterday," he replied.

They settled themselves at the shadiest table they could find and ordered lunch and a couple of beers.

"Well, what do you think?" she asked.

Steve didn't reply immediately. He slowly and deliberately looked around the square and at the open market hall with its intricate beamwork and medieval grain measures still in place. "I think it's fantastic," he admitted, still gazing around but particularly trying to adjust his eyes to the darkness in the furthest part of the market hall. "It's just a pity that it attracts all sorts."

"Now don't spoil things Steve. This is our day out, remember." She leaned across the table and squeezed his arm. He smiled back. So what if someone was watching them from the shadows? With a girl as good-looking as Annie, it was to be expected. Or perhaps he'd been mistaken.

Annie hadn't taken her hand from his arm. "Steve, this isn't really your scene, is it?" She looked at him with a serious, concerned expression. This girl really cared. Twenty years younger than him and a raving beauty. It just went to show that life could still turn up some good cards.

He put his hand over hers and linked their fingers together. "Don't ruin your day by thinking too much about how I feel," he said. "As far as I'm concerned we're here to enjoy ourselves, and that's exactly what I intend to do."

She nodded and slowly withdrew her hand, and they silently drank their beers. By the time their meals arrived there were few people left in or around the square. The sun reigned supreme; even through the heavy-gauge parasol over their table they could feel the rays beginning to prick their skin.

"If you've got some sun blocker I'm more than willing to rub it in for you," he said.

"What a shame I haven't," she replied. "I'm usually prepared for most things." Steve would have put money on that.

By three o'clock they'd finished off with coffee and cigarettes and Annie left him to see to the bill, saying she'd meet him back at the car. He eventually received the change when the young waitress, who was very presentable but with an utterly bored and morose expression, realised that he wasn't going to drift off and leave it. A pity she had an attitude problem; she wasn't without the necessary.

Although he didn't know the strength of her English, he couldn't resist making a comment. "Mademoiselle, flaunt them and smile. You never know where it might get you." She obviously didn't understand.

He now felt something of a heel trying to score points off her and he was pleased that Annie wasn't there to witness it. To try and make amends he pushed a twenty-euro note back on to her tray and left her probably more confused than before.

Annie had strolled off in one direction using the shadowed archways, but he saw little point in following; if she was meeting up with whoever had been watching them, it wouldn't be in full view of Joe Public. He took the other way, stopping only to admire a shop window full of antique clocks in various stages of repair, and within five minutes he was back at the corner of the square near the church. She was waiting for him in the car with a large carrier bag on her knees.

"Typical woman," he said, "as soon as the shops are open the spending instinct takes over."

"All very necessary, I think you'll agree," she said. "Some Reine Claudes, greengages to you, some factor fifteen and a torch."

She opened the bag for him to peer in. "Well we've just finished eating and you can hardly say it's dark yet. I reckon we should make a start with this," he said, pulling out the tube of lotion.

There were only half a dozen cars in the car park and none of them were occupied. Annie smiled. She gave an involuntary flinch of her shoulders when the cold cream touched her skin, then leaned her head back and closed her eyes. The smile remained as Steve stroked her shoulders and neck, then eased his hand down inside the low, scooped neckline of her blouse. He leaned across and kissed her on the lips and then between her breasts. She dropped her head forward and rubbed her face in his thick, black hair, then very gently but firmly took his hand away.

"Daytime's for exploring places, not persons," she said, in a teasing, matter-of-fact tone. She turned the ignition key and the engine growled into life.

"In that case I can't wait for it to get dark," Steve answered, straightening himself up.

Annie drove back up to the old gateway and from there took the D660 signposted to Beaumont.

"So now you're going to take me to a good hiding place. I couldn't have planned this better myself."

"This place is too cold and depressing for the sort of thing you have in mind," she retorted. "It's a huge underground munitions storage place that the Germans made during the war."

"And how far is it from here?" he asked.

"About ten kilometres. It's not quite as far as Beaumont, but I might have to search a bit for the entrance."

"That would surprise me."

She glanced quickly at him and then grinned as he leered back at her. And then, one hundred yards ahead, he saw a dark green Peugeot. He couldn't be one hundred per cent sure, but he just had the feeling that Annie eased off the throttle at the same moment. Steve forced himself to relax. It was probably just some local farmer who had decided to be different from the rest of them. One of the area's ubiquitous white Renault vans took the opportunity of their reduced speed to bounce its way past them, but that was the sum total of the traffic. Five minutes later they were coming off the low, cultivated plateau and were gradually losing height; a left-hand bend, then another, followed by a long downhill stretch. On the left-hand side the woods reached almost to the edge of the road forming a thick and almost impenetrable barrier. The other side was open; a shallow valley given over to grass.

"We're here," Annie announced suddenly, at the same time fiercely braking the car and slewing it onto the narrow verge alongside the field.

She pointed over her shoulder. Steve looked around and thirty yards back, he saw what might possibly be a faint track that seemed to lead directly into the close belt of trees and undergrowth. They both got out. Annie leaned back in for the torch and then she carefully locked the car.

"That's good thinking, Annie. I bet there's at least half

a dozen car thieves within a quarter-mile radius of here," he said mockingly, and then he thought again about the dark green Peugeot and the fact that he was now sure somebody had been watching them or him in Monpazier. It suddenly struck him. Who was it they had been watching – Annie, both of them, or just him?

There was no time to mull it over, as Annie had already gone up the road and was pushing her way through the bushes. He quickly followed, stooping to avoid low branches, and then, only ten yards into the wood, he was amazed to find himself in a clearing at the foot of a cliff about thirty feet high which had been completely invisible from the road. On the higher part of it brambles, ferns and small, twisted trees were somehow struggling to survive, their roots using all the natural cracks and crevices in the limestone. But the bottom half of the cliff just wasn't there – instead a huge, black square of an opening led into the solid rock.

"In the woods but not in the woods." He repeated her phrase back to her as they walked together into the opening. A strange greenish filtered light, coming through the tree canopy, reached in for about ten yards, but beyond that nothing could be seen.

For the first time that day Steve felt a chill creeping over him.

"Does that torch of yours work, or is it purely ornamental?" he asked.

"Sorry, I wasn't thinking." She switched it on and directed the beam around the walls.

"Mm, this is some cave," said Steve as he made a quick visual measurement. "I reckon two lorries could scrape past each other in here. Do you know how far in it goes?"

"No, but a fair way I think. I've only ever been as far as the chamber off to the side here. You can see where a wall was built across it to keep any undesirables out." As she spoke she waved the torch around to light up the remains of a breeze-block wall on their right. "It probably wasn't necessary though, as there were guards here all the time," she added.

Steve took her hand with the torch and directed it further into the main chamber. They slowly walked in for about fifty yards along a rock floor which, like the sides of the cavern, had obviously been machine cut. They passed two other side chambers but didn't turn into them, as if subconsciously they both wanted to keep the entrance visible behind them.

At a third side turning, Annie took hold of Steve's arm.

"I think I'd rather go back now," she said in a low voice, but her words were amplified in the confined area and there was also an echo from the side chamber. Steve flashed the torch ahead to see if they were nearing the end, but it seemed to continue at least as far as they'd already penetrated into the hillside.

"It looks as if it's all the same however far it goes," he said. "I've seen all I want."

They turned and began to retrace their steps and, although they were heading for the entrance which was straight ahead of them, they kept the torchlight on to light up the floor a few yards ahead of them.

"It's a strange place, isn't it?" remarked Annie when they were about halfway back.

"It certainly is," replied Steve. "I was just wondering what use could be made of it these days, in between O'Donnell stashing away his illegal arms of course."

"Wine, or mushrooms," she replied.

"Come on girl, where's your imagination? It's crying out to be used for sex orgies."

Just as she was about to reply he put his hand up to her mouth, switched off the torch and pulled her down beside a pile of broken breeze blocks. "Don't start anyth…"

"Listen!" he hissed in her ear. He was sure he had heard soft footsteps in the cavern other than their own. There was someone else in there, and not too far from them either.

As they crouched, silent, looking towards the square of daylight at the entrance, Steve was fairly certain that they couldn't be picked out unless whoever it was had a torch. He was even more certain that no one could get out of the cavern without being seen by them. It was a stalemate.

One minute passed, then two. Still no movement. Annie shifted her position a little to make herself more comfortable. Steve gripped her forearm firmly and shook it slightly, but he didn't speak. Three minutes, then four, with the only sound coming from a thin trickle of soil falling across the entrance, presumably disturbed by a small creature moving on the upper cliff face.

Then Annie again moved slightly, but this time she seemed to stagger as she crouched, and she pulled Steve across her. The torch blazed, directly into his eyes. As they both scrambled to their feet the sound of someone running from the cavern could be clearly heard. Steve looked, but his eyes, still blinded from the sudden torchlight, could only vaguely make out the figure of a man as he was silhouetted against the daylight at the entrance. Then he was gone completely with a frantic clattering through the trees.

"Thanks a bundle, Annie," said Steve, not trying too hard to hide the note of sarcasm.

"What do you mean?" she asked.

"For blinding me at the crucial moment."

"I couldn't help that. My legs were cramping up," she replied in an innocent and injured voice.

"Well somebody should thank you, because I think you might have saved someone from being killed."

"Let's get out of here," she said, and an involuntary

shudder passed through her shoulders.

"Yes. Let's get laid in Belvès without giving thrills to peeping toms." He took her hand. She made no reply.

Back on the road there was no sign of the person who had been in the cave. They reached the car and Steve drove off in silence, both smoking cigarettes. Steve wished he could have access to her thoughts.

They took the minor roads, passing through St. Avit Rivière and Bouillac, to return to Belvès. Steve drove and Annie navigated, but sightseeing was not on the agenda. At Belvès he parked the Volvo in the same area outside the Mairie.

At about the same time as they were walking across to their hotel, a dark green Peugeot was pulling up the slope into the centre of the town. It parked in the main square and a small, bespectacled Frenchman, with a remarkable resemblance to a prematurely-aged owl, got out. He walked, surprisingly quickly, down the Rue Jacques Manchotte, turned into the Impasse de Cours and let himself in through a door labelled 'R. Larequaie'. Sean O'Donnell was waiting for him.

CHAPTER FOURTEEN

Back in their hotel room, Steve got his wish at last. Annie did her horizontal best to make the early evening pass pleasantly for both of them, and her best was something special. Certainly Steve found no reason to complain, even though he knew it could only be an interlude before they were both hauled back into the main reason for them being there.

He was having a shower, mentally savouring the very recent past, when for him the interlude ended. He had just stepped out of the cubicle and started to towel himself down when the bathroom door opened. Expecting it to be Annie, he was more than a little aggrieved when Macbride appeared and pulled the door to behind him.

"What the fuck?" said Steve.

Macbride didn't speak, but reached in front of Steve and turned the shower back on. As he did so Steve was reminded of what people had said about Macbride in the past — that when he entered a room it darkened, and it wasn't simply due to his size. It was still true.

Steve recovered his composure as he started to pull on his clothes. "Well this is a nice surprise," he said. "And there was me thinking Annie had just remembered another move or two."

"Keep the sarcasm for some other time, Steve," Macbride said as he casually leaned against the door.

"Where is she?" asked Steve.

"I persuaded her to go down and have a drink with Lorenzo. Now listen, and concentrate. You forget Annie for the time being."

"And we were just getting to know each other," put in Steve.

Macbride's face hardened. "Steve, you listen to me. I've got about ten minutes and then I'll have to shift my butt."

"Am I right in assuming O'Donnell doesn't know you're seeing other men?" said Steve with a smile as he reached towards the cigarettes and lighter which he'd left on the glass shelf above the washbasin. Macbride, just as casually, eased himself forward and then shot out an arm and grabbed Steve's wrist.

"No lighters, Steve, remember? I'll give you a match if you're desperate."

"No problem," said Steve with a shrug. "I'm a health freak. I can go without one for at least ten minutes."

Macbride released his grip and Steve continued with his dressing, but neither of them relaxed. "You're right, O'Donnell doesn't know I'm here and let's hope for both our sakes he doesn't get to know," said Macbride. "I wouldn't have risked it if I didn't think it was necessary."

"Okay, don't pussyfoot around, just put me in the picture," said Steve. "At the moment it seems to me I'm just a courier who doesn't know what he's carrying or where he's carrying it to. But it also looks like there's quite a few interested parties who know more than I do and are just playing me along. And, would you believe it, that makes me feel decidedly pissed off."

Macbride pursed his lips and nodded. "Don't think I can't see it from your point of view but we've got problems," he admitted reluctantly. "This thing isn't working out as we'd expected."

"Your ten minutes is probably down to nine by now," Steve reminded him, "so let's have it."

"Yeah," agreed Macbride, "but you've got to hear me out. And remember it's pointless two of us being shit scared."

That in itself was sufficient to drive Steve into ultra-serious mode, as of all the things Macbride could be said to have, an intimate knowledge of fear wasn't among them. Certainly in his dealings with him in the past Steve had never seen any evidence to suggest he even knew the meaning of the word; occasionally puzzled, perhaps even moments of being mentally overtaxed, but never scared. If he was prepared to admit such a possibility, then they were indeed in deep and dangerous waters.

Macbride made his shoulders more comfortable against the door surround before continuing.

"About fifteen years ago a quantity of plutonium 239 in pellet form and more than 99.6% purity was stolen from the old Soviet Union research programme. It was thought North Korea and Iraq might be involved, but it just seemed to have disappeared without trace. Until August of last year."

"Then what?"

"German customs at Munich airport seized 300 grams of the stuff."

"Well done German customs."

"You would think so, wouldn't you," continued Macbride. "Although there wasn't enough to make a nuclear bomb there was enough, if it got into the wrong hands, to poison the water supply of half of Germany."

"You're not suggesting German customs is the wrong hands, are you?"

"Probably not, but somehow the 300 grams at Munich had turned into 250 grams by the time it had been transported to Solingen for safe disposal."

"Now that is unfortunate."

Macbride ignored the remark and continued. "Word has got round that the 50 grams has been split and that O'Donnell has a fair bit of it."

"And I take it there are various groups who think a few grams would make a good bargaining counter for their particular cause," said Steve.

"That's about it. Threat to water supplies, or the pellets could be burned to release a plume of smoke to irradiate the centre of a city."

Steve was puzzled. "There's no way this stuff can be carried in anything less than a lead-lined container, certainly not in a lightweight, modern camera."

Macbride raised his eyebrows and spoke slowly. "The camera contains a slip of paper with the grid location of where the pellets are. That's what you're carrying. Whether the location is correct is another matter. Lorenzo thinks it is. I don't know."

"But he's prepared to risk it," said Steve.

"Looks that way. But in the last twenty-four hours there's been a further complication, because another party has arrived on the scene."

"I'll have that cigarette," said Steve.

Macbride struck the match for him. "There are more terrorist groups around than there are packages of this stuff," he continued. "We now know that at least two of them have got wind of this operation."

Steve drew deeply on the cigarette. "You know I'm getting less and less interested in being involved in this."

"Your interest is of no consequence," retorted Macbride. "It's a job, you're contracted to it whether you like it or not. You've no option, you'll see it through. This is not the time to try to renegotiate."

It was said with a half smile, but Steve was well aware of the hidden menace in the words. Just for a moment, he thought of asking if Leila had tried to renegotiate, but he decided to let the matter ride. He knew, without needing to be reminded by anyone, that he had not been engaged for a walk-on, walk-off part.

"You've two minutes left," said Steve.

"Right," said Macbride. "We think O'Donnell might switch the route he's putting you on. If he does we'll need to know."

"He's brought you along so far, so where's the problem? You'll know as soon as I do. Probably sooner."

"I'm along so far, but he could drop me off any time. There's no way I can insist that he takes me all the way. But you're different. For him you're a key player."

"Okay. But if we assume I manage to see this thing through and then find you've been ditched along the way, who do I contact?"

"You don't," said Macbride, easing himself away from the door. "Somebody will contact you."

"One last thing," said Steve. "About these other parties you mentioned. Who do I watch?"

"You watch everybody. Annie, Lorenzo, Sean O'Donnell, Barloni. You haven't forgotten, this is not a trust profession."

"Would I ever forget that," countered Steve. "But there's two you've missed," he continued, speaking slowly and quietly and enjoying the look of puzzlement that came into Macbride's face.

"Who?" he demanded. Steve decided to chance his arm – he had nothing to lose and it just might hit some sort of mark. He felt in need of a confidence booster.

"A short, fat, elderly Frenchman who spends some time in an empty back shop when he's not chatting to Lorenzo or trying to keep tabs on me and Annie," he said.

Macbride's face was empty of emotion. He wasn't going to waste time expressing surprise or making contradictions, and Steve appreciated that, as he wasn't in the mood for any play acting.

"And who's the second one I missed?" asked Macbride. Steve looked him squarely in the eye; this he relished and he smiled, but only with his mouth. "Do you really need me to spell it out?"

"Excellent," said Macbride. "Together we just might see this thing through." As he pulled the door open he continued, "Have a pleasant evening with Annie and don't...."

"Don't say it," broke in Steve.

"Don't forget to turn the shower off." This time a genuine smile lit up his heavy features. "See you in the morning. We start at eight."

After he'd gone, Steve finished his cigarette before going back into the bedroom. Annie wasn't there. He presumed she was still being entertained by Lorenzo, and he felt a sudden pang of jealousy.

He strolled across to the window, but there was no sign of Macbride. In the small, shrubbed area beside the Mairie several young folk, male and female, had gathered around the wooden benches. It was obviously a meeting point, as at that moment they all moved off in a group and made towards the town centre. He could hear their cheerful voices and laughter and even feel their general youthful, carefree excitement, which sparked a long-forgotten chord. He suddenly felt a melancholic sense of loss and he remained standing there, staring out at what might have been, even after the last of the group had disappeared from his sight.

He was brought back to the present a few minutes later when Annie returned.

"I saw Macbride leaving the hotel," she said. "Are you any wiser now?"

"Wiser? Now that I don't know," he answered. He looked at her, but for the first time he didn't really see her. "Let's say I heard what Macbride told me."

"Who's talking in riddles now?" she asked, arching her eyebrows. Steve perched himself on the arm of one of the chairs and was deep in thought for a few moments before answering with his own question.

"If you were Macbride, or O'Donnell, or Lorenzo, or however many more of them there are, what would you expect me to do for the rest of this evening?"

Annie walked across to stand behind him, placed her hands on the top of his shoulders and gave a gentle squeeze. "I think they'd expect you to have a pleasant meal in the restaurant here with a good bottle of wine and then back up here for, well… an early night," she ended, smiling.

Steve nodded in agreement. Then he took her hands in his and pulled her gently round to be in front of him.

"Please don't take this as a personal affront," he said, "but the early night part of your plan might have to wait." She made to protest, but he stood, gave her a quick kiss, and made for the bathroom. "Be ready to go down in ten minutes, okay?" He didn't wait for her reply.

Ten minutes later they were in the hotel's ground floor restaurant. There were two other couples already there, so Steve ignored the table the waiter was directing towards and chose one close to a window looking out onto the street. Outside the evening was drawing in quickly and the few street lights were showing as suspended pale yellow spheres, which, rather than illuminate the area, did more to accentuate shadowed walls and dark doorways. Certainly from where they were sitting the entrance to Rue Jacques Manchotte looked more like the entrance to a tunnel than to a street.

If this was meant to be the hoped-for pleasant, relaxing part of the evening then both of them were very disappointed. The food was very good and the wine, a Jaubertie chosen by Annie, was even better, but the place was singularly lacking in atmosphere. Conversation on both sides was stilted, awkward and anything but sparkling, and, as a result, Steve found himself anxious for the meal to come to an end. He decided unilaterally that they should skip coffee and Annie, as keen to move on to something different as he was, made no protest.

"You've now got a simple choice, Annie," he said, after he'd dispatched the hovering waiter.

"You mean I either stay in the hotel and worry like hell about where you are and what you're up to or I come with you," she replied. "That's not much of a choice, is it?"

"Believe me, it's not what I had in mind earlier." He smiled. "But either you go up to our room and get our coats or you wait here while I get them."

"And if I do you'll be sniffing around for the luscious Rita," said Annie. "Don't think I've forgotten your reaction when you first clapped eyes on her."

His smile turned into a grin. "I'll get the coats," he said, and strode off for the stairs. He was gone longer than Annie had anticipated and she found herself having to studiously ignore the curious but surreptitious glances from the other couples. Eventually he reappeared with her light green knee-length coat over his arm.

"Did you have a problem choosing for me from my extensive travelling wardrobe?" she asked.

"I had to attend to something," he answered. "In any case, whatever I brought you'd look great in," he added as he helped her into the coat.

There was no sign of Barloni or Rita as they made their way through the lobby. As soon as they were outside the hotel he hurried her across the road. He was pleased to see that there was no one around, and even the café bar on the corner had shut up for the night; luck was on his side again.

To Annie's surprise, instead of turning into the main street as she'd expected, he directed her down a narrow footpath. This led to the back of the shops and Steve was sure that it would take them up to the turning where he'd followed Lorenzo that morning.

"For someone who says he's never been here before you certainly seem to know your way around," said Annie, hanging on to his arm. Every few yards she was having to put in three short, running steps to keep up with Steve's pace.

"When I went for the coats I had a good look at the

plan of the town that's hanging in the lobby," he lied. For some reason he couldn't have explained, he still felt it was to his advantage that she shouldn't be aware of how he'd followed Lorenzo earlier in the day.

"So where are we going? I mean a girl really should know before she goes down a dark, back alley with a sex-crazed male," she said, still having difficulty keeping up with him.

"Thanks for the compliment." He slowed his pace and Annie, mistakenly, took it to be a sign of consideration, but in fact it was because he was searching for the narrow gap that would give them access to the Impasse de Cours. He hadn't approached it from this direction last time, so there were no even half-familiar landmarks to assist him. However, his distance estimation was good and in a further twenty yards they were there.

He stopped at the corner, held Annie firmly by the arm, and listened. In the near-blackness every sound seemed amplified, even their breathing. Some distance away a dog barked frantically and then the sound subsided into a mournful whine, while much closer to them a scuttling rodent set their neck hairs on edge.

Annie put her lips to Steve's ear. "I'm not too happy here," she whispered. He placed a forefinger across her mouth. "It's not for long," he replied. Bending down, he blindly felt along the junction of the path and the wall they were standing against and found some small pebbles. He flicked them around the corner so that they bounced and scattered along the gap, making a noise which, he thought, surely couldn't be ignored. He was right, because, almost instantly, a strong torch beam flooded the entrance and lit up the rectangle of alleyway just beyond where Steve and Annie were now standing motionless. The beam stayed on, swaying slightly, for several minutes, as if the holder of the torch was considering his next move or simply plucking up courage to investigate further.

Then soft footsteps started to move slowly towards the corner. They stopped just short of where the pair stood. Steve squeezed Annie's arm and pulled her down into a crouching position beside him. There was no sound for what seemed an age, but was probably no more than a minute. Then the footsteps started again but this time receding, their owner apparently satisfied that all was well. He couldn't have been more wrong.

Steve stood up and peered carefully round the corner. The man was about ten yards away and he'd kept the torch on to light his way back to the main street. Silhouetted against the thin light coming down from the street, Steve could make out the figure of a small, rotund man. He would have been prepared to put money on it being the Frenchman who had been in the town square that morning and also probably in Monpazier and then the cavern near Beaumont only a few hours ago. The opportunity to get some answers to nagging questions was too good to miss.

"Stay here," he whispered into Annie's ear and moved swiftly and silently around the corner. It was indeed the Frenchman, and he was completely unaware of any danger until Steve's shoelace looped over his head and tightened on his thick neck.

Steve knew the wire within the lace was well capable of doing a cutting job, so he used restraint – he needed to have the man conscious. With the lace still held firm he pushed down on the man's shoulders, forcing him into a sitting position. He crouched beside him, recovered the torch, which had rolled from the Frenchman's grasp, and turned the beam full onto his face.

"Do you speak English?" he rasped, but even as he did so he had the feeling that this guy's speaking days could already be over. The man was not moving. He felt for the carotid pulse; nothing.

"Blast," he hissed to himself and silently cursed his luck. He knew the wire hadn't been tight enough to do a throttling job; the shock must have triggered a heart attack. At that moment he didn't have an ounce of sympathy for the Frenchman, just a seething fury that he should have chosen this particular time to expire. Not only would his questions remain unanswered, he was going to have to extricate himself and Annie from a potentially difficult situation. He rapidly took the loop of lace from the dead man's neck, switched off the torch, and then returned to the corner where Annie was waiting.

"What was all the commotion?" she asked. Steve didn't answer. He simply took her arm, turned her round and headed both of them back towards the hotel. His brain was racing, trying to think of some way out of this particular mess, but he couldn't come up with any sort of story that might hold water in the morning.

"Annie, if you're asked, we were never up here. Okay? We strolled around the lower part of the street, that's all."

"Okay," she answered," if that's what you want." She knew better than to argue or ask for explanations.

As it happened his request didn't surprise her, as she had glanced around the corner and seen Steve shining the torch full in the face of the elderly Frenchman. She had also seen him taking the lace from around the slumped man's neck.

Back at the hotel, Steve insisted that they should spend some time drinking in the lounge bar. From past experience he knew that most people when questioned were better on placings than timings. To establish that they had spent some time there before going up to their room might be of some use if there was any sort of hue and cry in the morning.

★ ★ ★

Later that evening it was Macbride who literally stumbled over the body of the Frenchman in the alleyway beside his flat. He immediately recognised Steve's handiwork or, more correctly, the handiwork of someone who had been trained by McKenna. Larequaie was no great loss, but the body couldn't be left where it was, nor could it be simply transported elsewhere, as any close examination of the neck would bring a major police involvement. It was O'Donnell who came up with the lorry plan.

CHAPTER FIFTEEN

Steve was certainly wrong about the possibility of there being some sort of hue and cry in the morning, unless one accepts that twenty minutes past midnight is morning. That was the time when their bedroom door was opened, using the hotel's spare key, and Lorenzo and Macbride noiselessly made their way into the room. The first thing Steve was aware of was being hauled up by the shoulders and the beam of a pencil torch shining into his screwed-up eyes.

Annie, lying beside him, jerked herself up into a sitting position with a startled gasp and pulled the blanket up to her neck.

"No need for modesty, Annie" said Lorenzo. "Use the bathroom. We've got a little bit of business to attend to here, and it doesn't concern you." Annie needed no second bidding. Steve heard the bathroom door open, then close, and then it was Macbride who took over.

"Steve, you're coming with us. There's been a development, and there's a job you can do for us."

"At this time of night? What sort of job?" Steve asked as he tried rapidly to unscramble his sleep-sodden senses.

"Nothing to worry about." If Macbride thought he had put a reassuring tone into his voice, he was wrong. "It's really just a bit of tidying up that O'Donnell wants taken care of," he continued. "He reckons you're the one to do it. Pull a few clothes on. You'll be back in half an hour."

"Now that at least is reassuring," muttered Steve, as he pulled on trousers and sweater over his boxer shorts. He took a little more care with his shoes and Lorenzo, losing patience, flung the jacket at him that he'd taken from the back of the chair.

"We haven't got all night," he snarled.

When Steve stood up, as ready as he could be, Macbride half opened the bathroom door and called in, "You can go back to bed, Annie. And don't worry, he'll be back in one piece."

It was getting better by the minute, thought Steve, but there was no time for further thought as he was bustled out of the room by the other two. He heard the door quietly pulled to until the lock clicked and then he was pushed along the landing in the direction of the emergency exit. From there metalled stairs ran down to a small, fenced yard at the back of the hotel. The yard was used as a depository for large unwanted items as well as being the storage area for refuse bins, so Macbride had to use a shaded torch to guide them through.

At the yard gate he stopped them for a moment, but there was no sound of anyone else being on the move. From there they moved round to the front of the hotel. Moonlight was showing fitfully through fast-moving, high-flying clouds, but one of the street lights was still on, providing some further illumination. However, its candlepower, which hadn't been good earlier, was now made even poorer by a huge swarm of flying insects which clustered around its globe. Steve had assumed that they would be going up the main street, but as he made to go in that direction, he was surprised to find Macbride striding off towards the car park beside the Mairie. He glanced at Lorenzo and it was obvious that that was where all three of them were going.

"Thought he might be taking a stroll round the block by himself," he said. "Sort of constitutional."

At first he thought Lorenzo hadn't heard him or just wasn't going to bother to reply until, as they were crossing the road, he responded, "We go that way as well." It was spoken in a tone that implied no frivolity – this was serious stuff.

They passed the shrubbed area where he had seen the young people congregate earlier and crossed the car park. The Volvo was where Steve and Annie had left it on their return from their day trip, and there were half a dozen other cars including a Citroen 2CV. It suddenly struck

Steve that this might be the vehicle that had been brought out at the airfield; the one which, at the time, he had thought was for Lorenzo. He wondered why it hadn't been parked nearer the centre of town, where Lorenzo obviously had contacts.

However, it didn't seem of any importance now as Macbride led the way past all of them and turned into a small street which ran along the far side of the large four-square stone building. A lorry was parked half way along the street facing them, its huge bulk almost filling the roadway. Macbride reached up and opened the cab door, which was not locked, then hauled himself up and in. He shuffled across and squeezed past the steering wheel, into the passenger seat.

"Okay, now you Steve," he called, and indicated that the driver's seat was for him. Steve pulled himself into the vehicle and, once he was settled behind the steering wheel, turned to Macbride.

"No room for Lorenzo up here?"

"That's right. In any case he's got some arrangements to see to. And now I've got you here," he continued, his voice dropping to little more than a whisper, "for Christ's sake stop acting as if you can influence things. You're a courier for them. Do that job, others will do theirs."

He pushed the ignition key into Steve's hand. "I take it you haven't forgotten how to drive one of these things," he said, his voice back to its normal volume.

Steve inserted the key, turned it, and, with a deep growl, the engine rumbled into life.

"Where are we headed?" he asked.

Macbride smiled grimly and gave him a friendly but vigorous slap on the shoulders. "Nice one Steve, I like it. Nothing like a bit of humour to lighten up the proceedings."

As Steve checked his side mirror, he saw a shadowy figure straightening up from around the offside rear wheel area of the lorry. The figure turned and he saw that it was Lorenzo. A sudden chill hit Steve as he had the first inkling of the tidying-up job they were involving him in.

"Just take it slow and easy," instructed Macbride. "We don't want to wake the whole town up. From here go out onto the main road, turn left, then down the hill and the garage where we got it from is about fifty yards on the right. We'll leave it there and then stroll back to our respective beds. Couldn't be easier, could it? Now let's go."

Steve quickly went through his options. He came to the conclusion that in total they came to only one better than zero. A cold sweat broke out over his back as he engaged first gear, slowly let in the clutch, released the handbrake and eased the lorry forward. He felt the rear offside wheel gently rise, as if a small rock had been placed in front of it. A glance in his side mirror confirmed his suspicions. Lorenzo was still there, but now he was crouched down examining something with the aid of his pencil torch. Steve wasn't able to make it out, but he knew it wasn't a rock.

"This is an elaborate way of killing a corpse," he muttered to Macbride as he turned the lorry onto the main road.

"We couldn't have him being found where he was or the way he was, and he couldn't just disappear," answered Macbride. "This way it's a tragic road accident, they have them here as well you know. There'll be no trace of your wirework."

There was no further conversation during the drive to the garage, which only took a few minutes even at the crawling speed Macbride insisted upon. They parked on a small area of wasteland behind the main garage building.

"Well, you can get back to Annie now," said Macbride, as he jumped down from the cab, "and don't take any detours. We'll see you at eight. Be ready."

As he was about to stride off, Steve grabbed his arm. "One thing before you go. Why didn't you or Lorenzo drive the lorry? Why me?"

"O'Donnell's idea. I think he just wanted to impress on you that he's the one calling the shots." He pushed his face close to Steve's. "It would be a good thing if you remembered that. It might save us all a lot of grief over the next few days." He then walked rapidly back up the slope towards the square and was swallowed up by the darkness.

Steve slowly made his own way back towards the hotel. He was in no hurry; he was anxious that his footsteps shouldn't be too loud in the deserted street, and he also needed time to mull over the whole episode. Perhaps it could be explained away as Macbride had said. However, if Macbride was lying, what other solution could there be? Was he being protected or set up, or were they ensuring that nothing would interfere with the present scheme? Lorenzo was very much involved. And hadn't Annie said that he was one hundred per cent O'Donnell's man? According to Macbride, that might not be the case now. Perhaps he should heed Macbride's advice and play the courier.

He had now reached the corner of the shrubbery and the hotel was in sight. Suddenly, for no reason he could have given, he decided to inspect the result of the night's work, macabre though it might be. As he turned into the car park the air seemed colder than it had been twenty minutes earlier. The side street was deserted, except for a large stray dog which suddenly materialised out of the blackness ahead of him. It made a jump to one side when it saw him and then, ears and tail down and with a curious crouching run, it disappeared down a narrow cut between houses. It had come from where the lorry had been parked, and Steve surmised that it had come across the body and was running in fear and shock at its discovery; after all, it had probably roamed this area for years and was accustomed to it being corpse-free.

Steve steeled himself to continue, and twenty yards further on he came to the body. It was not quite where he had expected it to be, but he assumed it had been dragged a little by the lorry, or perhaps even by the dog. But it wasn't that which almost had him following the fleeing dog. Looking at dead bodies which had come to sudden and bloody ends was not a new experience for him, although he hadn't had to do so for a long time. But being mentally prepared and ready to examine a particular body and then finding that he was not looking at the body he expected was something else.

There was no doubt about it – the body was not that of the plump, elderly Frenchman. As he gazed down at it, a thin rift in the cloud cover allowed a wan light to reach into the lane, sufficient to show that this was a much bigger, heavier man. He bent down, and as he did so the moon sailed free of the cloud. What it revealed was not pleasant. The body was lying on its back and the face was simply a squashed blood and flesh-coloured mess; any identification from the neck upwards would probably defeat the most expert and painstaking reconstruction work. But from the neck down the body appeared to be unmarked, and Steve had no doubt that he was looking at the corpse of Signor Barloni.

He straightened up and decided he'd seen all he wanted to see and, more importantly, what he was sure that they, Macbride, Lorenzo or whoever, hadn't wanted him to see. If he was looking for any crumb of comfort at that moment that had to be it; but this wasn't the place to be hanging around – any thinking would be best done well away from there.

In the short time it took him to get back to the hotel room, he'd decided on his next move. It involved far more risk than he would have wished, but all the alternatives seemed worse. For the first time in his life he was going to have to depend on a woman to help him through; if Annie didn't see her role fitting into his game plan then he had big problems. All he could do was sketch the outline to her, then trust her and not trust her at one and the same time.

"Stay lucky, Steve," he whispered to himself. He took the back stairs to the hotel and then quietly let himself into the bedroom. Annie was wide awake; she had been anxiously waiting for his return. She pushed herself up in bed.

"Where did you go?" she asked as he draped his jacket round her shoulders. She smiled and snuggled into it. If he was looking for confirmation for his proposed course of action, that smile went a long way towards it.

"Are you really awake, Annie?" he asked, "because you need to be, if we're going to be of any use to each other."

"Isn't that always the case," she replied sleepily, but then she caught the seriousness of his tone and sat up further. "I am awake and listening," she said, her eyes now wide open and full on him.

★ ★ ★

Macbride had sought out Lorenzo to move Larequaie's body to the Mairie car park while he borrowed the lorry. It was the stroke of good fortune that Lorenzo needed, as he too had the embarrassment of a body to dispose of. He used the 2CV to transport both Larequaie and Barloni to the car park. By the time Macbride had brought the lorry round, both bodies were ready, but that of Barloni was hidden in the deepest shadow beside the wall. As it turned out Macbride didn't bother to look at how Lorenzo arranged things.

They then collected Steve from his slumbers once again and got him to drive the lorry over Larequaie's head. Then, while Steve and Macbride were driving the lorry back to the garage, Lorenzo heaved Larequaie's body into the boot of the 2CV, checked that the car was fully locked, and then threw the keys into the shrubbery. He reckoned that by the time the body was discovered they would be long gone.

CHAPTER SIXTEEN

Very quickly, Steve told Annie what had occurred during his time away from the hotel with Macbride and Lorenzo. He recounted the incident with the lorry and told how he had later checked the body and found that it was almost certainly that of Signor Barloni, although he spared her the graphic details. If she hadn't unscrambled her senses before, she had now. With a grave face, she hung on his every word and, to Steve's relief, she didn't interrupt him with any questions.

He paused for a moment, aware that this was the crunch time when he would have to lay himself wide open and put her trustworthiness on the line. Almost absentmindedly he ran his fingers through her hair, then twisted his hand which caused her to give a little yelp. He took a deep breath before making the final commitment.

"I want you to believe me Annie, when I say that I would rather walk away from this whole crazy set-up if that was an option. But it isn't. None of those involved would allow that. So the only sensible course is to go through with it."

He stopped there, although it was obvious to Annie that he hadn't finished. She nodded, but her frown suggested that she was simply agreeing with his assessment so far and was not committing herself; she did not yet know where it was leading.

"But?" she ventured.

"Yes, the second but," he replied, still stroking her hair, which sparkled red in the light from the bedside lamp. "And this is where you've got to accept that unlike you, not everybody is driven by principles."

"Steve, I've been around long enough to know that. It's no great revelation. I'm well aware that not everyone has been fortunate enough to have had a convent upbringing."

"Well that's good to hear. So it won't worry you that I don't give a tinker's toss which side comes out on top as long as I've thrown my lot in with them." Again he hesitated a moment, trying to gauge her reaction, before he continued. "It seems to me the way things are panning out that it has to be the side that you're on."

She had pulled her knees up to her chest and put her arms around them. She was still listening intently, but the frown was still in place. He wasn't receiving any vibes at all; it was all high risk, high wire stuff now and if there had been any sort of safety net before he felt he was about to remove it.

"Put me right in the picture Annie and all my shots, not just the best ones, will be for you," he went on.

She didn't reply immediately but dropped her head so her face was hidden from him. It was her turn for risk assessment, and she was no happier with it than he had been.

"You really mean that?" she said.

"As never before," he replied, hoping his expression was the epitome of honesty and steadfastness. It had to be enough; she had to be convinced, but he had little else to put to her.

"But you're assuming I know," she said, her face still turned from him. "You're assuming I can put you in the picture, even if I wanted to."

Steve grabbed both her arms and made her sit up so she was looking at him. "Annie, for fuck's sake, stop the play acting. I've said I'll throw in my lot with you, but I expect you to be straight with me. I don't trust any of the others."

"Not even Macbride?" she asked, with a slight lift of the eyebrows and a faint, rueful smile.

"Perhaps least of all Macbride," he said as he released her arms. "Well, what do you say?"

She didn't answer. Instead she pulled the bedclothes aside, stepped out of the bed and went across to her jacket, which was draped over the chair. Even in that moment, when his thoughts were racing over the problems of the situation they were in, Steve couldn't help but admire her beautiful figure and her easy, lithe movement. She stirred his libido as no one else had done for a long while. He desperately hoped she would comply; he would get no pleasure from destroying her.

She came back to the bed, held out an opened cigarette packet and sat down beside him. He took two cigarettes, lit them both, then passed one to her.

"Is this meant to calm my troubled nerves?" he asked, with a grim smile.

She looked at him in a quizzical fashion. It was obvious that the debate within her was still not completely resolved. But he knew he couldn't rush her; if this was to work it had to be a decision made by her in her own time.

"Maybe," she answered, "because I think if you're not very careful you could be in a lot of danger."

"Go on, surprise me."

"Well, Lorenzo and I are both working for O'Donnell, as you already know," she said, looking directly at him, as if trying to assess his reaction, before dropping her gaze down to her clasped hands. "We don't know why you had to be brought in, but we suspect that Macbride is becoming unreliable and O'Donnell is using you to check this out."

"So what you're saying is that as long as I keep my side of the bargain I'm okay. It's not me who's got the problem, it's Macbride." He took a long drag on his cigarette, then exhaled a thin stream of smoke towards the ceiling before adding, "Where's the danger in that for me?"

"I wish it was as simple as that," she answered. "I think once O'Donnell has satisfied himself about Macbride, one way or the other, he will consider you to be expendable, like Leila. And I don't want that to happen." She leaned forward and placed her hands on his knees.

"That's just what I wanted to hear," he said and covered her hands with his. "And as from now, Lorenzo may be your partner, but he'll be my buddy if that will please you."

"Very much," she answered, pulling her hands from his, then putting them round his neck and kissing him.

"With one proviso," said Steve, reluctantly disentangling himself from her.

"What's that?"

"I have plans for you, so he'd better not chance his arm, or any other part of his anatomy."

She smiled and Steve felt himself being drawn again into the spell of her sparkling eyes.

"Steve, you're hopeless. But you're also very nice. In any case, you've no need to worry on that score. Lorenzo has other interests and they're not the same as yours." She twisted her face and made a slight movement of her hands to indicate that she was not making judgements, simply stating a fact. "But he has been a good friend to me," she added.

"Takes all sorts," said Steve, leaning across and kissing her on the forehead and then on the lips. "Now let's get organised so we can get on our way."

"There's no rush. Macbride and Lorenzo said they'd pick us up at eight."

"True, but you seem to have forgotten that there are two bodies out there," he nodded towards the window, "and at least one of them is waiting for someone to trip over it in the morning. I don't think it would be a good idea for me to be around when that happens."

He didn't really believe O'Donnell would allow that to happen; the bodies wouldn't have figured in his plans, so he was sure they would already have been removed to avoid any possible complications. But that didn't alter the fact that the more alterations he could make to O'Donnell's arrangements, the more some advantage might shift to him.

"I want us to leave here as soon as we're packed," he said. "They won't know we've gone for at least five hours." He looked at his watch. "Enough time for us to make things difficult for them. And, by the way, where are we headed?"

"A place called Le Bugue," she answered, then added,

"you'll have to make that four and a half hours as I must tell Lorenzo." She quickly started to throw on her clothes. As far as Steve was concerned he would have been more than happy if Lorenzo had been left out of the picture, but he couldn't think of any objections to put to her that she might have accepted. He started to pack as Annie made for the door.

"Make sure you're back here in half an hour or I might decide not to wait," was his parting shot as she quietly closed the door on herself. It was an utterly pointless remark, a toothless threat, and he knew it; she would be back, as he still had the camera, and even if she wasn't, he had no transport. But he had felt obliged to make some sort of assertive gesture, because he instinctively knew that for at least the last five minutes, she had been lying through her teeth. Her leaving to inform Lorenzo simply confirmed this for him.

He forced himself to concentrate on his packing, particularly the camera, which he retrieved from behind the framed print at the far end of the corridor where he had put it when Annie had taken her shower on their arrival. He remembered then that Macbride had hinted that it might not contain anything worthwhile. Could it be the sprat to catch the mackerel?

He finished packing before allowing his brain time to consider the events of the evening, and also the conversation he'd just had with Annie. She'd said she was still working for O'Donnell, yet when he'd tackled her in the car on the woodland track just down from the airfield she'd said she was with Macbride. Now she was suggesting that Macbride might be suspect. It wouldn't be the first time such a thing had happened; Macbride was of an age where one big pay deal might prove to be irresistible. But if she was lying to him, and all his instincts told him that she was, then she must be working with Lorenzo, and the two of them must, at that very moment, be desperately rejigging their schedule to fit in with this earlier departure time from Belvès. If that was the case O'Donnell and Macbride would be four and a half hours late in starting and would not know where they were headed.

Self-preservation began to take over his thoughts. He had no desire to travel towards an undisclosed collecting group without any hope of back-up, no matter how remote a possibility that might be. Once the camera was handed over he would be of no further use to them, but he would be an embarrassment and certainly surplus to requirements.

He reckoned he probably had five minutes before Annie and Lorenzo arrived. In that time he scribbled a quick note on a sheet of hotel notepaper, sealed it in the envelope, and hurried down the back stairs down which Macbride and Lorenzo had led him only an hour or so earlier. The post box was attached to the wall of the Mairie, and it was the work of a moment to post the letter and then make his way back to the hotel room. He had done as much as he could, but whether Agnew, or whoever was now in his place, could or would make any sense of "Left Belvès by car, heading for Le Bugue 3.30 am". he knew might be stretching hope to beyond breaking point. It would have to be a question of "Stay lucky, Steve" yet again.

His trust in his star would have been greatly shaken if he had been aware that he had been observed. Rita's room was on the second floor of the hotel and she was sitting, awake and fully dressed, at the unlit window which overlooked the car park. She was more than a little intrigued to see him posting a letter at that time in the morning.

★ ★ ★

Steve's decision for them to make their move out of Belvès several hours earlier than planned was anxiously relayed to Lorenzo by Annie. Outwardly he took the news without batting an eyelid.

"Okay," he said, "if that's what he wants, go along with it. The Peugeot will be in the car park, take it. I'll get in touch with ETA and get them to bring things forward. I'm sure it'll not cause them any problems. And don't worry,

O'Donnell has no knowledge of my links with Cocteau. I'll catch up with you there."

Annie then left him to return to the hotel. She was not wholly convinced by what Lorenzo had said, but she felt that she was now on an ordained course; the die had been cast. But Lorenzo was not of the same opinion. He reckoned the die had not stopped rolling, and he could pick it up and roll again.

After Annie left him, he spent a tormented hour going over in his mind all the possible scenarios. Eventually he came to the conclusion that none of them would allow the plan he and Annie had concocted to work out as they'd hoped. There was only one decision left open to him.

★ ★ ★

The Impasse de Cours was as dead as the grave as he turned into it. Outside the door of number 1 he hesitated, but only for a moment, before pushing the illuminated bell. By now he had convinced himself that he was set on the only course of action by which he could save himself. There was no way he could help Annie now, she was dead meat.

The ring on the bell was answered unexpectedly quickly, and when he entered the room he was surprised to find that both O'Donnell and Macbride were fully dressed.

"At this time of night it must be important," said O'Donnell.

Lorenzo nodded. "I think so."

The two men listened without comment while Lorenzo told them that Steve and Annie were about to drive to the Cocteau estate somewhere near Le Bugue. And she had said that Steve still had the camera.

When he had finished O'Donnell remained sitting impassively for a time before smiling and turning to Macbride.

"You can now see how this man is so special to me," he said. Then to Lorenzo, "As always, you've done well. I know Cocteau and his estate from many years ago, before your time. There's no need to rush after them. We'll follow in the morning, but I think you should go with us, we may need you. Be here at seven."

He ushered Lorenzo out of the door. As soon as it was firmly closed, he crushed one fist into the other. "A good length of rope," he said to no one in particular.

Lorenzo made his way back to the room above the antique shop feeling distinctly disturbed. He had not been aware of O'Donnell having any previous contact with Cocteau; somehow he knew he would have to ensure that he couldn't be linked in any way with Annie's actions.

At much the same time as Lorenzo was grappling to come to terms with a situation that was increasingly slipping from his control, Rita, at the hotel, was struggling to overcome the inadequacies of others. After seeing Annie and Steve drive out of the car park in the very early hours of the morning she had tried to raise her immediate superior, Barloni, without success. Other officers of her rank who had been similarly placed in the other two hotels had by now been stood down as being surplus to requirements – the French security system was not so generously manned that they could afford to allocate unlimited resources to assist their Italian neighbours – so she had to work through the convoluted and at times tenuous links between local gendarmerie and regional security.

It was almost 8 am before she succeeded in raising the first glimmer of interest, and then suddenly the whole process became clogged by the discovery of a body in the car park; the body of her superior, Barloni. By then Sean O'Donnell, Macbride and Lorenzo were well on their way towards Le Bugue and, unknown to him, Steve's hope of some form of assistance was beginning to look extremely forlorn.

CHAPTER SEVENTEEN

Steve had thrown the rest of Annie's things into her bag and was just zipping it closed when she returned. To his surprise, Lorenzo wasn't with her.

"Where is he?" he asked. "Has he decided to opt out?"

"No. He knows where we're headed but he needs to consult with others and make some arrangements," she explained as she rapidly checked that he had not missed any of her things.

"There are such things as phones, you know," he suggested gently.

"Would you want a call at this time of night?" she retorted. "He said he'll wait until breakfast time, but he thinks it's best for us to go now and he'll catch up with us later."

"Okay, I'm with you," said Steve, in as easy and carefree a tone as he could manage. It belied his real feelings. "Let's go," he added, picking up both of the bags. He was keen to get on the move, not to lose any more of their time advantage and to put some distance between themselves and Belvès, although he was not at all happy that Lorenzo was staying behind to prepare the way. He would far rather have had him in his sights.

They made a silent exit from the hotel. Down in the Mairie car park, Annie led the way. She ignored the Volvo and instead produced the keys for a dark green Peugeot. It hadn't been there earlier, but Steve felt pretty sure it was the one that had tracked them to and from Monpazier, although he couldn't swear to it.

As they settled themselves, with Annie behind the wheel, she answered his unspoken question.

"Lorenzo dropped this car here for us. The Volvo's too well known. With this the others won't know what we're travelling in."

"Good thinking," said Steve approvingly, although he couldn't help wondering if someone was just trying to lull him, or them, into a false sense of security.

As Annie pulled out onto the D710 and headed north he would have had even more cause for concern if he had been aware of Rita noting their departure and then starting to make the first in a series of urgent telephone calls.

Away from the tightly built-up area of the sleeping town, the night was very black. They made their way down a long, winding road, passing the garage where Steve had left the lorry. Along the valley bottom, fog lay thick over the river and thin tendrils of it stretched over the road, merging in places, to make driving difficult with the car's headlights reflecting back off it. Annie was forced to drive at a more sedate speed than she would have liked. Steve had little option other than to trust her driving, so he sank back into his seat. As far as he could make out they didn't seem to have wakened the dead by their early morning departure, so he reckoned he could doze in peace for a while; after all it had been a long, trying day and this might be the only chance he'd get to charge up his batteries.

Annie took a quick glance at him, then gave all her attention to her driving. Fortunately she'd travelled the road several times before, although not in fog and not in these circumstances, and she was aware of the growing tension within herself. But she made reasonably good time until they reached the outskirts of the town.

Tuesday was market day in Le Bugue and with a few kilometres still to go, they found themselves in a slow-moving convoy of assorted vehicles laden with agricultural and horticultural produce; the transit vans bringing in clothes and crafts would arrive later.

By the time Annie drove across the high, multi-arched bridge there was already much activity in the Place du Marché, with stallholders setting out their displays. She turned left, taking the road around the flag-bedecked Hotel

Royal Vézère, and then pulled into a small parking lot outside the recently-renovated mill building which housed the Office du Tourisme.

"Making a phone call, back in a minute," she called to him as she switched off the engine and jumped out of the car. Steve didn't bother to reply, as she was already making her way down a shallow ramp leading to a batch of phone cubicles. He reluctantly roused himself from the semi-dozed state which he'd allowed himself to drift into on the drive and opened his door slightly to let the early morning air drifting up from the river help in the waking process. Once he was fully conscious, his eyes were drawn to the posters of tourist–orientated attractions which were plastered on boards on both sides of the broad, stepped walkway leading to the main building and on its glass-panelled doors. Among them the smiling Les Vagabonds group were prominently featured – obviously on a grand summer tour taking in Le Buisson, Le Bugue, and Ste. Alvère among other places over the next three weeks. Good luck to them, he thought.

He turned his attention to the other buildings in the immediate area. Straight ahead was an inviting-looking *logis*, the Hotel du Cygne, and, across a small lane from that, was the Station de Pompiers with its full complement of assorted gleaming vehicles standing proudly on its forecourt. On occasions in the past, the distant past, he had

had reason to be indebted to the resourcefulness of firefighters and he felt sure that if the need arose the *sapeurs-pompiers* would show similar qualities to their English and German counterparts. He took it as some sort of omen that the town had a manned fire station, as he knew that not all of them had.

Other than those buildings there was nothing else of interest in his line of vision, but in any case Annie was now making her way back to the car. She was looking relaxed, and he even noted a spring in her step.

"It's all fixed," she said. "It's going to work out. There's no one using the cottage, so it's all ours."

"With a welcoming bottle of wine and the bed already aired?" he asked with a grin.

"If there is, you can help yourself to the bottle. After the night I've had the bed will be most welcome, aired or not," she replied as she started the car. Before slipping it into gear she stared vacantly out through the windscreen, apparently about to say more, then changed her mind.

The town seemed to be a lot smaller than Steve had expected because of the number of market stalls. Within minutes they had left behind the last of the houses which straggled along the cliff road overlooking the wide flood plain of the meandering Vézère before it joined the Dordogne. The road twisted away from the river and ran through typical Perigordian landscape; wooded hill slopes with massive, horizontal limestone outcrops showing through in places and small cleared areas where large, brown cattle grazed and even smaller areas devoted to a dozen yards or so of black, stumped vines.

About ten kilometres along the D710, just past the junction to Limeuil, a larger tract of hillside had been cleared. There were neither animals nor crops and it was separated from the road by a double line of high, close-meshed wire fencing.

"This is the start of the Cocteau estate," said Annie, nodding towards the fenced land. "The cottage we'll be staying at is in there, on the far side of the hill."

As she finished speaking they arrived at a double set of wrought iron gates set into the fencing. The wire fences at this point were about ten metres apart, and in the space between the gates was a small, stone building looking every inch the guardhouse that it obviously was. From it a young man emerged as the car pulled up at the first gate. He could easily have been mistaken for a rugby front row forward, but the slight bulge which spoiled the line of a beautifully cut suit suggested that if the occasion demanded he wouldn't have to rely solely on his physical attributes.

In military fashion the man marched smartly to the gate where, he waited, making no move to open it. Annie got out of the car and the two of them had a short conversation in rapid French before he went back into the building and operated the gate mechanisms. Only one gate opened at a time, and as soon as they had driven through the first it closed before the second opened. It then closed behind them silently and, Steve felt, ominously.

"Don't you just have the feeling that those gates and the fences and that guy are now all there to stop us getting out, not to stop anyone else getting in?" Steve asked.

Annie started the vehicle up the well-maintained tarmac drive which took a diagonal line across the cleared hillside. She smiled, but kept her eyes fixed on the road ahead.

"You've got too much imagination, Steve. You'll be thinking the worst of these dogs next, and really they're just pets." As she spoke four huge black dogs came racing down the drive towards them. Apart from their size and the speed with which they covered the ground, the most impressive and frightening aspect was their chilling silence. There was not a single bark between them. It didn't take the slightest bit of imagination for Steve to see them as exactly what they were; a trained team of killers. He found himself automatically checking that his door and window were tightly closed.

"What sort of brutes are they?" he asked, looking at them almost mesmerised as they wheeled around the car and then, as if on some pre-arranged signal, turned and loped easily up the track two on each side of the vehicle.

"Bas-rouges," answered Annie, "see their red socks? They're a bit like a cross between a Doberman and a Rottweiler, but they are a breed in their own right. They're also really sweet unless told to be otherwise," she added.

Steve didn't pursue the conversation but continued to stare at the dogs as they trotted alongside. He just hoped he would not be around when they were told otherwise.

The car crested the rise. On the other side of the hill a long slope led down through beautifully-kept parkland; manicured lawns were interspersed with patches of variegated shrubs and several large specimen trees. At the foot of the slope stood a superb three-storey mansion with a walled terrace on the side facing them.

"Don't tell me that's the cottage," he said.

"Lovely isn't it," she replied. "But I'm sorry to disappoint you. The cottage is about another hundred yards further on. You won't see it until we get round the house."

She rolled the car slowly down the drive and then pulled in beside stone steps which led up onto the terrace. To Steve's consternation all four dogs reappeared and milled around the car, but Annie seemed not to have noticed. "Do you have to stop here right in the middle of this pack?" he asked, trying to keep any trace of anxiety out of his voice.

"Before we go to the cottage we'd better go in here to meet the man who owns all of this," she explained. "It's politeness and we're expected."

Although he didn't say it, Steve had no intention of meeting anyone outside while the dogs were loose. Partly to delay the moment when he would feel obliged to leave the safety of the vehicle, he asked the name of the owner.

"Monsieur Cocteau will do," she answered, "He is Cocteau d'Euskadi, of the Basque country. But I'll tell you more later." She finished off quickly as a middle-aged woman appeared at the top of the steps. She shouted something to the dogs, which, to Steve's intense relief, raced off round the back of the house but once more in their close formation. She then came down the steps and welcomed Annie as if she was a long-lost daughter returning home.

Steve got out of the car slowly, as if not to intrude on the welcoming, although in truth he was checking to make sure the dogs hadn't decided to set their own agenda.

"This is Michelle," said Annie, before they made their way up onto the terrace and then across to an open doorway which Steve noticed had at some time been almost doubled in width. "She would have you believe that she is nothing more than a glorified unpaid housekeeper, but I could tell you a tale or two," she continued.

"Shush with you. He might believe you," was Michelle's reply, with a slight rising of colour in her cheeks. She spoke English with an attractive foreign accent that Steve couldn't place.

From the terrace level they entered the house, stepping down two small tiled steps alongside which was a non-slip metal and rubber ramp. The room had evidently once been a kitchen area, as the massive fireplace still had the roasting spit, now an ornamental feature, and the huge old beams of the ceiling were festooned with an array of different-sized hooks. It was now comfortably furnished with expensive leather settees, three of them, and one wall was completely taken up with two large display cabinets containing collections of porcelain and silverware.

The floor of the room was completely bare of coverings, not even a small rug, but the reason was soon obvious. There was a tall table to the side of one of the settees, and sitting at it in a wheelchair was an old man who Steve guessed must be ninety if he was a day.

"Father, you remember Annie? This is a friend of hers."

Michelle glanced at Steve and waited for him to complete the introduction. Steve stepped forward, noticing as he did so that the man had had his left leg amputated just above the knee.

"I'm Steve Cromarty, sir. I'm from England," he said as he proffered his hand. The old man nodded but made no reply and made no move to shake hands. Instead he turned his chair so he was facing his daughter and spoke to her in a quavering voice and in a language that meant nothing to Steve. Michelle listened in a manner that made it plainly obvious that what her father decided was the law in this house and no argument would be brooked. When he had finished, Michelle turned to Annie and Steve.

"He says you are very welcome and you'll find all you need in the cottage. He'll meet you again at dinner over here and he'll talk with you then. But he has some business to attend to now."

At that the old man turned his wheelchair and, without another glance at any of them, touched a button to start its electric motor and steered himself out of the room through a doorway on the far side of the fireplace. Michelle shook her head sadly and a scowl of irritation crossed her face. Then, as if suddenly remembering that there were others present, she drew herself up, smoothed down the front of her dress and turned again to Annie. She handed her a key.

"I've got things to see to as well," she said, "but you know your way around, where you can go and where you can't. I'll see you at dinner, six thirty on the dot as always."

Annie and Steve returned to the car. For an awful moment it crossed Steve's mind that she might suggest they walk to the cottage, so he was much relieved when she drove them the short distance. He found it altogether too easy to bring to his mind's eye the sight of the four Bas-rouges; they were the stuff from which nightmares were not only made but could come true.

Once in the cottage they quickly had their clothes stowed and were sitting in the easy chairs with mugs of coffee in their hands. Annie's tired features reflected the fact that she had driven through part of the night along misty, unlit roads, but Steve couldn't let her go to bed before she put him more in the picture.

"I can see that Cocteau de whatever is a very wealthy man," he began. "It's also very obvious that he wields a lot of power. But I get the feeling it's not because of his money. Am I right?" Annie nodded. "So before you rest your pretty head I want you to tell me about him."

"I'm tired," she protested.

"And I'm waiting," he insisted.

CHAPTER EIGHTEEN

Annie drank off the rest of her coffee while Steve curbed his impatience and waited. It was very quiet in the room. She took a deep breath, then began.

"Michelle's father is a Basque. I take it you know of them?"

"Only that they come from an area that straddles the border between north-east Spain and France and some are French and some are Spanish. And at times they've earned themselves something of a bad press."

"You're only half right. That's what most people think," she said, then added firmly, "but they're not French or Spanish. They're all Basques, and very proud of it. They are the longest-established people in Europe and they have their own language, Euskera. Michelle and her father were using it when we were in the house with them."

"Okay, I'm impressed. But if he's so keen on his ancestry, why does he choose to live here instead of somewhere in Basqueland?"

Annie was not amused. She shot him an angry look and answered sharply, "Don't ever be flippant about his homeland. He may be old, but he has power." She gazed into her empty cup, her knuckles showing white as she gripped it.

"Right, I've got the message." Steve spread his hands. "No more wisecracks. Just tell me about him."

"Well, he's lived here in France since 1937 when he escaped from Durango - that's a town in the Basque area of northern Spain. You've heard of Durango?"

Steve shook his head. "It rings no bells with me, but I take it I should know of it."

"No, probably not. It's not very well known, although they would be appalled if they heard me say that. But I presume you have heard of Guernica, yes?"

He nodded. "I'm not completely ignorant, you know. Picasso made a painting of it, didn't he?"

"Yes," she continued, "everybody has heard of Guernica because of Picasso's painting, but very few know that Durango was bombed by the Luftwaffe with General Franco's approval a month before Guernica was terror-bombed."

"So Cocteau did the sensible thing and moved out, is that it?"

"There was more to it than that," said Annie quietly. "He lost his leg in that bombing and from what Michelle has told me, I think that made him more nationalistic than he had been before. During the Civil War in Spain the Basque leaders moved into Biarritz in North East France and set up government in exile, and he was an important member of it. After the Second World War ended in 1945 the other members returned to Bilbao and normal politics, but for some reason he didn't go back with them. Instead he moved here. It may have been because of the treatment he needed for his leg, but I don't really know. And it's not the sort of thing you can ask about, is it?"

"Not really."

"Anyway, in 1959 he was very much involved in the setting up of the ETA movement or, to give it its full title, Euskadi Ta Askatasuna. It translates as Basque Fatherland and Freedom. ETA was opposed to Franco's dictatorship but even more importantly, it was committed to fighting for a separate Basque state. Some say he's been the mastermind behind much of their activities ever since."

"Now ETA I have heard of," put in Steve, "Spain's equivalent of the IRA. So what you're really saying is that he has a nice little number going involving kidnapping, car bombing, and whatever else."

"I didn't say that, so don't try to put words into my mouth. But I do know he is very proud of having been the architect of the Basque revolutionary tax which has financed everything else that the movement has achieved so far."

"Including everything here, I should imagine," said Steve, who saw no reason to feel as well disposed towards Cocteau as Annie obviously was. "The estate, the house, his collections. Not bad for a man of principle, eh?"

"A man like him has to keep up appearances," she said, defending him. "He wouldn't be able to function efficiently if he didn't."

Steve didn't agree with her, but this was neither the time nor the place to debate the matter. Instead he gave her a non-committal smile.

"So, he's a powerful man but in his time, he must have made many enemies."

"I suppose so," she agreed. "Hence the security, which we only saw a fraction of because we were expected."

They fell silent, each with their own thoughts. Through half-lowered lids Steve watched Annie; although tired she was still looking remarkably relaxed, and he wondered if this place was to be the final dropping point. If that was so, then the time when he would become surplus to requirements might be rapidly approaching. In which case it was essential that he should find out more about the estate, even if that meant running the gauntlet of the dogs. Also he needed to know about the out-of-bounds areas that Michelle had referred to when they had left her to make their way to the cottage. He tried to keep his voice casual as he put the question.

"What did Michelle mean, about you knowing the places where we can and can't go?"

The question pulled Annie out of her reverie. "On the far side of the big house there's a small factory-type building. It's hidden from the house by a screen of trees. That's the main out of bounds area," she explained.

"Why? What's so special about it?"

"I don't know," she said, shaking her head. "I've never been there and I've never asked, but once Michelle did mention that it was a sort of foundry place. I think several men work there, but I've only met one of them. He's called Thierry and he told me he was trained as a bronze caster making statues and things like that. You know, the sort of things they put up in public squares. But I don't know if he was just trying to impress me."

"Couldn't blame him, but if he does have that sort of skill he would be a useful bloke to have around. Like an upmarket odd job man," said Steve. There was a derogatory hint in his tone, but he kept his other thoughts to himself. Conventional munitions work was based on foundry products, and here was a private foundry located in the sealed grounds of a known anti-Spanish government sympathiser.

"Anyway, I don't think it's got anything to do with us," she said, breaking into his thoughts. "Also we should be grateful to Michelle's father for letting us stay here and at such short notice."

Steve found it hard to believe that Annie would really think he'd fall for that. There'd be no way that Signor Cocteau would have allowed strangers into this complex of his unless he thought it was to his or ETA's advantage.

"Don't you worry yourself," he said. "I'm not going to go sniffing around. There's those damned devil hounds for a start, never mind social niceties."

"Good," she answered and gave a wide yawn. "Now I intend to get some sleep. I'll ring across and get them to give us a call at five so we're not late for dinner." She came across and kissed him on the forehead. "And don't forget I drove us here while you slept, so to make sure I get some rest I'm having the front bedroom and I'm locking the door. You, my precious, have the back room."

She smiled down at him, sliding both her palms down his cheeks, before she left him. However, she did not leave a desolated man behind her. Even just a few hours before he would have been cudgelling his brains to come up with an excuse, any excuse, to share a bed with her, but not now.

He heard her make the phone call, and then he gave her a further ten minutes to get settled. Then, in case she did reappear, he went to the back bedroom and made the room and its contents look as though he was intending to sleep there. He was unsure what to do, except that doing nothing was too negative to contemplate. But he did know that he was not at all comfortable being a pawn in a chess game being moved around by others. If he was to emerge from this situation unscathed it was going to be as the result of his own efforts, as he couldn't see where any help could come from.

He decided to wait another thirty minutes before doing anything, to make sure Annie was asleep and to allow himself more time to think, so that when he did act it might have a better chance of being to his advantage. "I'm too old for this," he muttered to himself. He was younger than Macbride, a hell of a lot younger, but Macbride had never stopped working at it, never had to try and pick up the discarded pieces and then wonder if he still had what it took to put it all together again.

He pulled himself up short. "Think like that and you may as well lie down and cash in your chips right here," he reminded himself.

He made a quick, silent search of the kitchen. It provided him with less than he'd hoped for, but he consoled himself by reckoning anything was better than bare hands if he was unfortunate enough to meet up with the dogs.

He listened carefully at Annie's bedroom door before making his way out of the front door of the cottage. The car was parked outside, and as he crouched down behind it he was completely hidden from the main house. It took him only a couple of minutes to ease the corner of the front bumper out sufficiently for him to wedge the camera behind it. He then went back into the cottage, pausing once more to check Annie's door, then went straight through and left by the back door.

It was still early, a little before nine, but there was already more than a hint of warmth in the air and the cloudless blue sky suggested that there was a scorching day in prospect. He fervently hoped that the dogs had decided to lie up.

There was a small paved area outside the door, then a patch of parched lawn. He strolled across this, confident that no one could object to him being there, and then he was in the shelter and shade of a copse of young trees. Standing there, he was able to see the side and back of the main house and also a large extension which had been built in the same yellow-grey stone as the original building. Beyond it he could just make out the roof line of a low building which was almost completely hidden by a thick, but trimmed, hedging of conifers. At each end of it there were short, metal chimneys, and he felt sure that it was the foundry Annie had mentioned – one of the out-of-bounds areas.

He suddenly remembered that he had meant to ask her which other areas were barred to them, but that would have to wait. To be on the safe side he would have to assume that he wouldn't be welcome anywhere he went now. He wasn't really into self-analysis; he'd seen too many people have their metaphorical heads chopped off while they were examining their metaphorical navels to convince him of its value. So he would have had difficulty trying to explain why he wanted to check out the foundry. Probably because it was there, and the cussed side of his nature didn't allow him to readily accept being excluded without being told why, and also because of a growing feeling that he was trapped – the Cocteau estate was a prison. If that was the case, then while he still had some degree of freedom, he thought he should find out what he could, as it just might come in useful later.

Keeping in the shelter of the trees as far as possible, he slowly made his way round towards the foundry.

CHAPTER NINETEEN

The Cocteau estate lay quiet, as if beaten down by the heat. On the ground nothing seemed to be stirring, but high above the hill they'd driven over that morning to reach the house and cottage a buzzard effortlessly soared, the light so clear that Steve could see the upward curve of its wingtips. He watched it make two long, slow circles before it moved off to scan another area, and he wondered if he would be more successful in his search than the bird.

From where he was standing, most of the back of the main house was visible. The large ground floor windows all had black scrolled ironwork across them; very decorative, in the Spanish style, but failing to disguise their main purpose. If Cocteau didn't consider the double fencing round the estate, armed guards and dogs to be sufficient to give him peace of mind, then he was obviously a man obsessed with his own protection. But then aren't we all, Steve reflected. The only real difference was that

Cocteau had the resources to do something about it, while the rest of us could only try to paper over the cracks.

He had answered his own question, and that brought him up sharp. He had to become more outward focused; allowing himself to be caught up with drifting thoughts was not the way out of his present predicament.

The possibility of entering the house unobserved seemed too risky, so he turned his attention to the extension he'd seen earlier. It was single storey and completely windowless. As he edged his way further through the trees he saw that it was linked to the nearer end wall of the foundry. He presumed it had been built to allow M. Cocteau safe and easy access to the work area using his wheelchair. Steve guessed there would be another entrance to the foundry, to allow raw materials to be brought in and whatever they were making to be taken out.

He was about to make for the further end to check it out when he heard the sound of approaching voices. He hurriedly pushed himself back into the copse of trees. Fortunately the stillness of the air and the absence of other sounds made them seem closer than they actually were, so it was a few minutes before they came into view. When they did he broke out in a cold sweat, thinking what might have occurred if he had met them on the open ground between the trees and the foundry.

There were three of them, young men who could have

been clones of the gatekeeper, and they had with them, on thick chain leads, the four Bas Rouges. The voices were clearly audible now, speaking French, and he could hardly believe his ears or his good fortune.

"It's too hot to walk them round," said one of them. "We'll put them inside the fences for the morning. Nobody will be any the wiser." Then they all disappeared from sight round the end of the foundry.

Steve, silently giving thanks to whoever it was who was looking after his star that morning, waited ten minutes to make sure the beasts were well and truly fenced. Confirmation of his good fortune came when, as he was about to move on again, the three men reappeared, minus the dogs, and sauntered back in the general direction of the house.

Within five minutes Steve, still moving cautiously but much more freely now that the threat of the dogs had gone, reached the end corner of the foundry and was in sight of its main door. He knew it was too much to expect that it would have been left open for him to have full view of the interior, so it was no great disappointment to see that it was closed. It was a large, thick steel sliding door with a smaller Judas door fitted into it. Above it a short length of girder jutted from the stonework with a pulley and wound chain attached to it. All of this was much as he'd imagined it would be, apart from the general tidiness around the place.

What he hadn't been prepared for was the large, gaping hole of a tunnel about thirty yards beyond the further end corner of the foundry building. The entrance to the tunnel was stone-faced, but even from where he stood, he could see that the inside was solid rock which had been machine cut. The rock was the same as that used on the house to foundry extension, so he assumed that the two jobs had gone hand in hand. He estimated that car-sized vehicles would be able to use the tunnel. Apart from being smaller, it looked much the same as the one Annie had taken him to see, what seemed months ago but in fact was only yesterday, near Beaumont.

Strange, he thought, that when he'd asked Annie if she could think of any possible use for the place she'd never thought to mention what Cocteau had done with this one. Either she genuinely didn't know or she was playing her cards very close to her shapely chest.

He wondered where the tunnel came out, but the idea of going in there to find out did not have much appeal. He would have to be in pretty desperate straits before he closed off his options in there. The foundry itself was a different matter. He was curious to know what was produced in there, but that was really just academic. What mattered more was for him to see if there was anything that might be of use to him.

He was now concealed by a thin belt of conifer hedging. He was assessing the risk involved if he were to boldly walk across and try to open the door when he heard the muffled sound of approaching vehicles. Almost immediately a convoy of three small white Renault vans – the ubiquitous vehicles of the region which had never been known to cause a head to turn – drove out of the tunnel and parked alongside each other just to one side of the foundry door. Two men got out of each van. One of the six unlocked the small door and they all stepped through into the foundry. Moments later Steve heard bolts being drawn back, and then the main door was slid open on its rollers. The men then made several journeys to and from the vans carrying in large, and obviously heavy, boxes.

Steve was well hidden, but his own view was very restricted. To see more he would somehow have to get himself into a position behind the vans, and to do that there was open ground that would have to be crossed. He could hear the men working in the foundry, but at odd intervals one or more returned to the vans to collect something from them. He decided it was altogether too risky, especially as he still had a few hours at his disposal before he and Annie were to meet up with the Cocteaus again. He reckoned there might be an opportunity when the men took their morning break; in the meantime he would make his way back to the cottage.

On the return journey he had to guard against complacency; things had gone so much his way up till now that the temptation to rush things was very strong. He wanted to get back as quickly as possible, but he successfully forced himself to take it slow and steady, and a good hour and a half passed between him leaving and now easing his way through the back door.

He closed the door with an almost palpable sigh of relief, but then he became suddenly conscious of a highly charged atmosphere, a mixture of fear and anxiety, that hadn't been there when he had left the cottage.

He moved swiftly into the living room, where he was confronted by Annie and Michelle. Annie had been crying; her eyes were very red and damp, and the way she was catching her breath suggested that tears were still not far away. She was sitting in an easy chair and Michelle was perched on one of its arms, gently stroking Annie's hair. This was certainly not the scene that Steve had assumed he was coming back to; the clangour of alarm bells inside his head at that moment was almost deafening.

"What's happened?" he asked.

Annie looked up in surprise; she appeared not to have heard him come into the room. She shook her head in a hopeless, helpless gesture and seemed about to speak, but the tears started to well up again and she covered her face with her hands.

Steve looked to Michelle. She was cool and calm. It would take a great deal to ruffle the feathers of that particular bird, he thought as he waited for her explanation.

"I'm afraid the bottom's dropped out of her world," she said, in a matter of fact tone, while continuing to stroke Annie's hair in an almost absent-minded fashion.

"How? Come on, put me in the picture," he demanded, dropping into the other armchair.

"There was a telephone call for my father about an hour ago," said Michelle. "His hearing isn't as good as he would have people believe, so I now take all his calls and then relay them to him."

She stopped stroking Annie's hair, and as soon as she did so Annie frantically took hold of her hand and pressed it to her lips and then her cheek.

"Tell him everything," Annie whispered. "He's involved. He should know." She looked across into Steve's face. "Please help," she added.

Steve knew that if her words and the pleading look in her eyes could make a heart bleed, then his should be pumping out all its eight pints. He nodded and attempted a smile, which did nothing for her, and waited for Michelle to continue.

"Evidently you are being followed here," said Michelle. "Sean O'Donnell, who had some business with my father a long time ago, is coming with two other men. He asked if Annie and you were already here and when I said you were he told me to tell my father to keep you here until he arrived. He said it was most important and that he would make sure the cause was not forgotten."

"Who could have told them that we were here?" asked Steve, looking at Annie. At first it seemed as though she couldn't bring herself to reply. Then, in a thin voice which was little more than a whisper, she said, "Only Lorenzo."

"So the scheme isn't going to work out after all," he said as gently as he could. "And that means the big pay-off and disappearing act are not going to happen." He was about to add 'at least for you', but thought better of it, not wishing to push her further into despair. But Annie had obviously thought that through for herself.

"Lorenzo must have decided to save his own skin," she said, with more of a sense of resignation than bitterness.

"If you could help, would you?" asked Michelle. The question, coming from her, took Steve by surprise.

"If you mean would I help Annie, the answer is a definite yes. But where would that leave you? Because it looks as though your father is going to be lined up with O'Donnell."

Michelle looked down at Annie before turning again to Steve with a sad, wistful expression on her face.

"For all of my life it has been expected that I would do whatever was best for my father and ETA," she said.

"Any dreams I might have had have always taken second place to their wishes. I have never been allowed to have any sort of life of my own." She stopped and again looked down at Annie before continuing. "He is a very old man now, and yet he is still prepared to cripple another young girl's life and I am supposed to go along with it for the cause. A cause, Mr Cromarty, that I do not now believe in."

"Not believing in the cause is one thing, but does that mean you would positively help us?" he asked.

She gave him a strong, firm look and then slowly nodded. "Yes, in any way I can."

"Michelle, how can I ever thank you, how can we ever thank you?" cried Annie, grabbing the older woman's hand again.

Steve broke in to ease Michelle's embarrassment, and to get back to considering their immediate situation.

"Apart from the main gate we came through, what other ways are there of getting out of the estate?" he asked.

"There's only one," Michelle answered. "It's a road tunnel cut through an old cave system. It goes from beside the foundry and leads out onto a track in the woods beyond the estate boundary. But it's only used for the foundry."

"And presumably it's guarded like the main gate," said Steve.

"No, there's no need. At the far end the tunnel is

completely barred off with two solid iron swing doors. One of the young guards who man the main gates and the perimeter fence goes down every working morning and unbolts them to let the foundrymen in and then bolts them again once they're in," explained Michelle. "They're never left open at any time."

"So if we could get down there we could open the gates. Is that what you're saying?" It was Annie asking the question, and Steve was reminded of the resilience she had shown in the apartment in Florence after Jason's murder. She was quickly recovering her composure.

"Yes," answered Michelle. "I could take you through the house and along to the foundry. From there you could take one of the vans, drive down the tunnel, open the gates yourself, and then make for the open road."

"Oh, you're a darling," said Annie, throwing her arms around her. Then, as suddenly, she pushed herself away as a thought struck her. "But what about you? What would your father say about it?"

"Leave me whatever it is you're carrying," said Michelle. "If I have that for father he'll not be interested in your escape. And this O'Donnell person and the others will just have had a wasted journey. It happens," she finished with a shrug.

A reasonable request, thought Steve, and said in such an off-hand, throwaway manner, and yet to him it sounded like nothing less than a spider inviting a fly to set the table for dinner.

Annie looked at Steve, as if seeking guidance, before answering. "I think we should. It's our only chance Steve."

"I told you at the beginning I was on your side, and that still applies. If the camera will get us out of this hole we're in then so be it."

"Excellent, Steve," said Michelle, using his Christian name for the first time. "I could take it now, across to the house; it'll be safe there."

"No," said Steve, to Annie's obvious surprise. "We'll keep it until we're on our way. Just in case your father comes up with an alternative plan." He added that to forestall any possible argument from Michelle. "Don't worry, once we're definitely on our way I'll let you know where it is."

A fleeting look of consternation had crossed Michelle's face, but she accepted his decision without further discussion. "Come across to the house at eleven thirty. That's when the foundrymen take their break. Bring whatever you're taking with you, because you won't be back here."

Annie and Steve agreed and Michelle left them as they began to reduce their luggage to a minimum. She had only been gone a short time when Steve told Annie that he had a job to do and would be back in half an hour. Annie, who had hardly spoken while they were repacking their things, showed surprisingly little interest and Steve thought she might be beginning to suffer from post-traumatic shock. He'd have to be particularly caring towards her, but that would be no hardship, and he looked forward to when he'd have the opportunity to make a start.

From leaving the cottage to returning to it actually took him twenty-eight minutes. First he retrieved the camera from the Peugeot and then, taking a risk at which he had baulked not much earlier, he managed to reach one of the vans parked outside the foundry and attach the camera to it. Then he rejoined Annie.

CHAPTER TWENTY

By the time he returned, Annie had finished sorting out the essential things she intended to take and she was slumped in a chair waiting for him. She was the picture of misery. Despite her natural resilience, the last twenty-four hours had taken its toll and the strain was etched on her face.

"Come on, girl, things are looking up," said Steve, in a tone that was far more light-hearted than he was feeling. She looked up at him and gave a wan smile.

"I'm not a child you know. You don't really believe that."

"It's true," he insisted. "Just give it some thought. We get out of here the way Michelle told us and then it's just you and me together."

"Yes, but till when?" she asked.

He bent over her, ran his fingers through her hair and kissed her brow. "The future's not there to spoil what we've got now," he answered.

"This is Steve the philosopher talking, is it?"

"That's right, we take each step just as it comes. And I reckon between us we've got what it takes."

"I hope so."

They fell silent, each with their own thoughts. Steve was aware that she was sinking back into her sombre, blue mood but he couldn't find the words to prevent it.

He was very relieved when it was time for them to make a move. At exactly eleven-thirty they walked across to the big house; there didn't seem much point in taking the Peugeot. All they had in the way of luggage was now on Steve's back in the daysack he had bought in Florence.

Up on the terrace, Michelle was waiting for them. "Full marks for punctuality," she said, pointing to her watch. She ushered them to a stone table with wickerwork chairs arranged around it. A jug of coffee and cups and filled glasses of orange juice were on the table ready for them.

"I thought you could have a drink here first," she said.

"But wouldn't it be better not to waste any time?" asked Annie.

"It's not wasting time," countered Michelle. "I need to make sure the men are on their break, out of your way."

"And what about the dogs?" asked Steve, who could still recall all too clearly the sight of them as they escorted them to the house that morning.

"Don't worry about them. They are never allowed here or in the foundry."

"What about your father?" asked Annie. "Isn't he going to think it strange us leaving like this without a word to him?"

"Remember, he's in his nineties," answered Michelle with a grimace. "He breakfasts in bed, then normally spends the rest of the morning doing whatever he has to do to get ready for his day, which starts early afternoon when he appears here. He was only here this morning because of your phone call to say you were arriving. He was back in his bedroom before you'd settled yourself in the cottage. I don't expect to see him now much before four. By then I'll have thought of something."

Annie poured coffee for herself and Steve; Michelle refused any and went off to check on the foundrymen. While they were sitting drinking a sudden breeze sprang up out of nowhere and the leaves of large potted shrubs, arranged around the edge of the terrace, started to shiver and rustle. The sky, which only moments before had been a cloudless, brilliant blue, now took on a yellow, bruised appearance and the temperature dropped, giving a distinct chill to the air. Steve was reminded of the storm in Florence, and with that reminder came Macbride's warning to him that there were two packs running. Then later in Belvès he'd said another group had come onto the scene and that from then on he would have to watch everybody. And that included Annie.

He glanced across at her; she was still quiet, but was looking more like her old self. She was without doubt the most desirable creature he'd ever set eyes on. He vowed then that if they got out of this he would do his damnedest to get her to go back to England with him – he still had the money O'Donnell had given him.

Annie wasn't looking at him; she was gazing into the distance, lost in her own thoughts.

"It'll be better when we're on the move," he said to her, but it fell on deaf ears.

Michelle had been gone more than five minutes and Steve was becoming just a little anxious; they needed to be on their way. Before they'd left the cottage he'd checked the rooms, supposedly to ensure they'd left nothing of importance, but he'd spent most of the time in the kitchen. If they didn't move soon the pile of damp cloths he'd piled on the electric grill would start to blaze. He'd hoped they would be on their way towards the tunnel before the fire was noticed; a diversion would work to their advantage, but not if it occurred before they moved from where they were now.

He was beginning to rack his brains for possible contingency plans when Michelle reappeared.

"I think it's best for you to move now," she said,

without further explanation. Annie got to her feet and went to Michelle and flung her arms around her. "How can I ever thank you? You're a true friend," she said.

Michelle returned the embrace. "You know there's no need." Then she pushed her away to hold her at arm's length. "Till we meet again, Annie."

She turned and led the two of them into the room where they had met M. Cocteau that morning. From there they passed into another room which was, if anything, even more expensively furnished. It convinced Steve that over the years Cocteau, as well as raising funds for the Basque cause, had made damned sure that his own comforts were well catered for.

They then entered a long, windowless corridor which was obviously the extension he had seen leading to the foundry. It was lit by strip lighting at intervals along the centre of the ceiling. A handrail ran the full length, but other than that there was nothing. Michelle hurried them along it; their footsteps on the stone-flagged floor echoing back at them from the walls. There was no attempt at conversation by any of them.

The corridor ended at a heavy wooden door, wide enough to allow a wheelchair to pass through. Michelle slid it to one side to reveal a steel door which had a viewing grill in its lower half.

"Wait here a moment," she said, as she bent down and checked through it before cautiously pushing it open and then indicating for them to follow her. "I'll leave you here. The entrance to the tunnel is straight ahead beyond the far door. The men usually take about a quarter of an hour for their break, but say ten minutes to be on the safe side."

She turned to Steve and held out an ignition key. "This is for the van furthest from the door," she said. Steve made to take it from her, but she pulled her hand back. "Come on, this is no time for games," he said.

"This is no game, I need the camera," she retorted. "With that I can mollify father."

"And we need it to make sure we get out," answered Steve. She shot him a venomous look. "Don't worry," he added. "I'll leave word where it is before we get out of the tunnel."

Michelle was stunned; this had obviously not entered into her calculations, and she looked to Annie for advice or support.

"Trust him," said Annie. "Remember I'm with him."

"Yes, that's true," said Michelle with a forced smile, and she turned to Steve and handed him the key with a measure of good grace. "Be in touch," she whispered to Annie, touching her arm. She then stepped back into the corridor and pulled the steel door shut with a clang that sounded quite deafening in the foundry. It was a noise Steve felt they could have done without.

He and Annie stood motionless for a moment, half expecting the noise to bring the foundrymen rushing back. They didn't, and Steve took control. Hanging along the side wall nearest to them were what he'd hoped to see – sets of foundrymen's working gear, heavy-gauge, full-length, fireproof coats and hats made of the same material with thick, plastic pull-down visors. He took down two sets and thrust one into Annie's arms.

"What's this for?" she demanded.

"Not your colour I know, but put them on," he said. "We'll wear them until we get to the van and through the tunnel." Then, in answer to her question he added, "If anyone does see us it might just make them unsure and so hesitate and give us more of a chance."

They struggled into the clothes, which were even heavier than Steve had imagined, and he put up a silent prayer that they wouldn't be required to do any sprints in them. He looked at Annie and found it difficult not to laugh at her as her coat was so long on her that it trailed on the ground. But this was neither the time nor the place to indulge in frivolity.

"This could be the worst part, Annie," he said. "Give me a kiss to keep me going until we can find another bed to share."

Somehow she had perked herself up, and she managed

to give him one of those smiles that went right through him. Holding up their visors, they kissed.

"Now let's get out of here and get to the van," Steve said, leading the way past the line of small, glowing furnaces, each of which was surrounded by its own shimmering heat haze. The main door of the building was still fully open, and they reached it without any problems. They could now see the three vans, parked exactly where Steve had last seen them, and also the entrance to the tunnel. It was all as Michelle had said. Everything was going like clockwork, and that worried him.

He stopped Annie in her tracks and peered round the door. He was appalled to see three of the foundrymen making their way back, their break obviously at an end. A vague thought flitted through his mind that Michelle might have sent them, but he dismissed it. Whether it was true or not was of no real consequence; the fact was it was a problem they could do without. The men were about fifty yards from the foundry door and if he and Annie delayed any longer they would never get past them.

"Keep on my left side Annie," said Steve, "visors down and we walk to the van. Remember, walk. Come on!"

The temptation to run was almost overwhelming and he had to resist taking her hand. He could feel rivulets of sweat beginning to make their way down his back and he knew it wasn't solely due to the clothes.

They had almost reached the line of vans when they heard the first shouts from the men. "Keep going!" Steve hissed to Annie and then, when there were more shouts, he grabbed her hand and pulled her along. They reached the furthest van and, despite the bulkiness of the clothes, slid into the seats. He felt more sweat break out on him as he pushed the key into the ignition and turned it. If Michelle had intended to sell them down the river then this was surely the way to do it.

The engine caught at the second attempt and as it did so, he glanced towards the men, who were now running towards them. At a quick calculation he couldn't see how he would be able to turn the van round before they would be pulling the doors open and hauling them out.

Then suddenly they all stopped and began pointing. Turning slightly, he could see what had caught their attention – thick smoke was rising from the direction of the cottage and at that instant, flames could be seen licking through the smoke. The tinder-dry roof beams had obviously caught fire. As the foundrymen stood, unsure which way to move, he took advantage of their indecision and quickly turned the van, heading it into the mouth of the tunnel. The ground surface in the tunnel was good, certainly good enough for a vehicle being driven carefully, but Steve was far from being in careful mode and they bucketed down the steep incline, testing the van's suspension to the full.

"Slow down, Steve!" shouted Annie, as she clung to the dashboard, her knuckles showing white.

"Just hang on," he shouted back. "Remember there's a door to unbolt and open when we come to the end of this. We'll need time for that."

Annie said nothing more, but desperately tried to wedge herself further back into the seat. There was no lighting in the tunnel and the lights of the van were not good. The tunnel took an unexpected turn, and the front left side of the van scraped against the wall. Steve slowed a little. The last thing he wanted was to crash the vehicle and then have to try to walk out of this place – he could envisage the tunnel being the ultimate trap.

The ground had started to level out and then, a short distance ahead, they could see thin slivers of daylight around the edges of the tunnel doors. Steve braked and the van skidded several yards before coming to a shuddering halt in front of the doors. He got out, but left the engine running.

"You stay in the van!" shouted Annie, who was already on her way to the doors. Steve ignored that and ran after her. "You might not be able to manage it by yourself," he pointed out.

Together they eased back the four huge securing bolts. Annie would have found it very difficult on her own because of the encumbering foundry gear which she was still wearing, although she had thrown off the hat and visor. They pushed open the doors and it was just as Michelle had described it to them; a track led from the tunnel and curved away through thick woodland. It was obviously well used and the tyre marks of the foundry vans could be clearly seen.

Steve put a hand on her shoulder. "Back in the van Annie, we're on our way."

"But what about the promise you made to Michelle?" said Annie, not making any move.

"The camera? Do you think she's really interested?"

"Of course she is," answered Annie hotly. "You know that. It's for her father."

"True," he said. "Well I left a note in one of the other vans saying where she could find it. So the promise is kept," he lied.

Annie beamed at him. "I love you, Steve Cromarty," she said.

And those were the last words she ever said. In the same instant two men forced their way through the bushes at the side of the tunnel entrance while a third followed at a more leisurely pace. What happened next was imprinted forever onto Steve's memory. It was all over in seconds, but when he relived it, as he would many times, it was as if it had occurred in slow motion.

Lorenzo was just ahead of Macbride. He had a handgun, and he leapt forward and pressed it against Annie's forehead. She made no move, no cry, but a tired, resigned look registered at the same moment as he fired. A split second after she fell, a bullet from Macbride's weapon tore a huge mass of Lorenzo's skull away.

Even in the midst of this carnage Steve was sure then, and would never be convinced otherwise, that Macbride had deliberately waited for Lorenzo to fire first; that Annie had become a further addition to his list of expendables.

The third man appeared. It was Sean O'Donnell. "I think we'll leave them where they are," he said. "They can be Cocteau's problem."

Steve felt the bile rising in his throat. Forcing himself not to turn and look at Annie's body, he glanced down and saw that the front of the foundryman's coat which he was still wearing was covered with blood splashes from both Annie and Lorenzo. He tore it off and threw it down, and that very action seemed to act as a catharsis; the past was at least partly gone.

He followed O'Donnell and Macbride as they made their way along the track to the road, where the grey Mercedes was waiting. O'Donnell took the wheel.

"We're going to drop you at Périgeux," he said over his shoulder. "You can catch the TGV and be in Paris for an evening meal. We've booked you in to the Lavoisier-

Malesherbes. Macbride says you know it." Steve didn't answer.

The journey to Périgeux unwrapped like some unreal episode in another person's life. But their final words to him, when forty minutes later they dropped him outside the station, made him realise that the unreality could well become the norm again.

O'Donnell leaned out of the driver's window. "A messy ending but a very satisfactory outcome. Stay lucky, Mr. Cromarty."

"We'll be in touch," Macbride softly called to him.

The car pulled away and he walked into the station entrance without a backward glance.

CHAPTER TWENTY ONE

Steve, overwhelmed by an awful sense of loss, remembered little of the journey to Paris. Again and again his mind ran over all that had happened since he had taken the Alitalia flight to Pisa en route to Florence. It seemed to him that the only possible point where he could have made a different choice was when he had decided to call into the Irish pub that first evening. But deep down he knew that they would have had alternative plans to ensnare him; he had been drawn back into the murkiest of worlds, one where loyalty and trust were at the whim of dangerous causes.

He stayed overnight as planned, at the hotel Lavoisiers-Malesherbes. He was in no particular hurry to quit the country; only Macbride and O'Donnell knew his location, and in any case, now he no longer had the camera, he didn't consider himself a target. He also felt in need of some time to allow the event at Cocteau's estate to become less harsh, less of a wound. An afternoon stroll away from the crowded Boulevard Haussmann into the tranquillity of the Parc Monceau started the healing process.

★ ★ ★

Two days after the deaths of Annie and Lorenzo, Steve was turning the key in the lock of his flat. He had been away little more than a week, so there was only a mini-mountain of unsolicited junk mail to resist the opening door. He shuffled it around with his foot to make sure there wasn't something worthwhile lurking there. He was half hoping there would be another insulting letter from his bank manager; with the money from O'Donnell safely tucked in his wallet, he would feel more than justified in telling him to stick wasps up his arse. But there wasn't.

He also noted, with a grim smile, that there was no note pinned to the inside door jamb as he continued on into the living room. Everything was as he had left it, except for the newspaper spread out on the small coffee table in the centre of the room. On it, held in place with a heavy ashtray, was a large, bulky manila envelope.

He tore it open and was thumbing the wad of notes when the telephone rang. It was Macbride.

"Welcome home Steve. You'll see from the envelope's contents that I put a good word in for you."

"Bollocks. I know you, Macbride."

"Forget it. Effusive thanks just embarrass me." There was just the slightest hint of lightness in Macbride's tone. "But I thought you might not have seen the article in the paper. I'll be in touch, probably sooner than last time." He rang off.

Steve put the envelope and the notes in his pocket and picked up the paper. It was the previous day's edition. A short article near the bottom of one of the centre pages had been ringed with a black felt pen marker.

From our Western Europe correspondent

French police confirmed today that the body of the man found in the burnt-out wreckage of a car which crashed in a remote area of northern Aquitaine had died from a single gunshot wound to the head and that a weapon had been found alongside the body. There is strong speculation that the body is that of Sean O'Donnell, who was being sought by authorities in both France and Italy in connection with drugs and arms smuggling. A spokesperson, who refused to be named, said it was thought that no other person was involved.

Knowing what he did of O'Donnell, Steve could hardly believe he would have turned the gun on himself, but if the French police were happy to take that line he could understand it; he certainly wasn't going to shed any tears.

He carefully folded the paper and waited. The phone rang, and this time he let it ring four times before he picked up the receiver.

"Nice and tidy, eh?" It was Macbride again.

"You always were fastidious," answered Steve. "And don't forget to let me know the funeral arrangements."

"Very thoughtful," said Macbride. "Your choice of flowers will be interesting."

Steve rang off. He was not in the mood to trade banter. He lit a cigarette, dragged deeply on it and blew a thin stream of smoke towards the ceiling while he tried to sort out his conflicting thoughts. One day there'd be a similar newspaper report about Macbride, of that he was sure, but he couldn't help himself hoping that it wouldn't be for a good while yet. And it wasn't just the money that made him wonder when the next call would come.

ND - #0474 - 270225 - C0 - 203/127/21 - PB - 9781861514547 - Matt Lamination